World Soul

Sergei Arefyev is a brilliant scientist at the Institute of Telepathy. Torn by a sense of isolation and alienation, he dreams of a human future where telepathy allows mankind to share its experiences fully. His dream seems to be fulfilled by the World Soul, a biological mutation that links human consciousnesses through telepathy. Lies and deception become impossible, wars can no longer be fought, and people experience an ecstasy of full communion with each other. However, human relations change dramatically as the lack of individual privacy leads to a loss of personal identity. In the midst of this turmoil the World Soul evolves until it acquires a will of its own, and Sergei and his friends must face the horrible challenge of reestablishing individual autonomy before mankind is completely engulfed.

TRANSLATED FROM THE RUSSIAN BY

Antonina W. Bouis

INTRODUCTION BY

Theodore Sturgeon

World Soul

Mikhail Emtsev and Eremei Parnov

COLLIER BOOKS
A Division of Macmillan Publishing Co., Inc.
New York

COLLIER MACMILLAN PUBLISHERS
London

Macmillan Publishing Co., Inc.
866 Third Avenue, New York, N.Y. 10022
Collier Macmillan Canada, Ltd.

Library of Congress Cataloging in Publication Data
Emtsev, Mikhail Tikhonovich, 1930–
World soul.
Translation of Dusha mira.
I. Parnov, Eremei Iudovich, 1935–   joint author.
II. Title
PZ4.E557Wo [PG3479.7.M7]   891.7'3'44   77-10908
ISBN 0-02-536020-5
ISBN 0-02-019850-7 pbk.

First Collier Books Edition 1979
Printed in the United States of America

Introduction

What an extraordinary novel this is!
It is good fiction.
It is good science.
It is fabulous!

To be good, fiction must score high on several scales of excellence. It must be well written, a portmanteau in which are packed such treasures as vivid imagery, characters a reader can care about, and that rare skill in story-telling which produces episodes transforming "I have read about it" into "It happened to me." It must provide both insights into the known and verisimilitude—believability—in its incursions into the unknown. Above all, it must be useful, in the broadest sense: entertaining in a way that justifies every moment of irreplaceable time the reader gives to it, educational both as to new knowledge and new ways to use knowledge.

Emtsev and Parnov succeed on all counts.

Good writing about science must also meet several rigorous criteria. It must inform, and inform clearly. Where it is about known phenomena, it must inform those of us who happen not to know without insulting us, and at the same time it must not insult those of us who do. And if it extrapolates, if it hypothesizes, plunges into the not-yet-known, it should do so off some thoroughly familiar springboard. Further, it is the duty of writers on scientific matters to fight one more battle in the never-ending war against the layman's confusion of science with technology, scientists with technicians. Finally, it is, in my intensely prejudiced opinion, an immoral act to explicate scientific matters, large or small, while disregarding the effects, or possible effects, of science on those who have to live with them—effects on the psyche, on politics, on philosophy, on the very nature of the human spirit.

Every word in this book is written with this special skill and this essential awareness.

"Fabulous" is as degraded a word as "love" ("I love raspberry sherbet; I got some yesterday at this fabulous place on Fourth Street"), which is a pity. The word derives from "fable" and, properly used, denotes the quality which separates living, lasting literature from merely competent fiction. The creation of fable is by no means the exclusive province of Aesop and La Fontaine. Scarlett O'Hara is a fabulous character, as are Scrooge, Hamlet, Oedipus, Charlie Brown, Lancelot, and the Red Queen. Places can be fabulous: the Garden of Eden, Poictesme, Mordor, Ruritania, Lilliput. And the intrusion of fantastic inventions, monstrosities, phenomena, like H. G. Wells's food of the gods, Martians, cometary dust—fables all. A fable is a tale that has a meaning larger than itself which illuminates the human condition (or predicament) inspirationally or as a caution.

And in this context, Emtsev and Parnov give you their "biotosis," a fabulous construct if ever there was one.

These Russian authors have, among their many deft dealings with the unexpected, a way of regarding any of their main characters as being, if not expendable, at least as subject to deadly peril as anyone else in the book. Not since Norman Mailer shot his hero through the head halfway through his first novel have I been so jolted as I am at what happens to some of the people herein contained, and it has made me wonder whether our Western convention of the "angle" character, the character from whose point of view the story is told, is necessarily a good thing. It is self-evident that a first-person narrative runs a serious risk of canceling suspense (how could "I" be telling the story unless I had survived the action?), and usually some artificial manipulation must be used to maintain the point of view. But isn't the use of an "angle" character the very next thing to this? One wonders whether that widespread conviction that deadly things can happen only to other people, never to oneself, is the product of this convention. If the bulk of our fiction had expendable protagonists, might we have less of that insane arrogance which permits us to drive without seat belts and smoke in bed? Anyway, be warned; all the people in this novel are up for grabs, and what happens to some of them will wring your heart.

These authors exhibit the most astonishing ability to move freely from profound examinations of the heart and mind to wide-screen visualizations of the social macrocosm and alternative futures. Look at this passionate passage, in which Sergei says to his Ruzhena:

Love, loving, it's all nonsense, Ruzhena. Love is closeness, deep and eternal. Nobody's ever known it. Adam and Eve, Romeo and Juliet—a beautiful lie that managed to crawl into the twentieth century. And what it was they really had, nobody knows. But for us . . . for us it's all complicated. When we are silent we understand many things. We are part of each other. But as soon as we utter a single word, we create a thought, and it separates us. Do you understand? The thought becomes a third person. It may not be superfluous, but it is the third. And sometimes it *is* superfluous. We don't feel each other, don't see ourselves, we only see it—the thought. Do you understand? I'm not

talking about a real third person, like Erik or Karabichev . . . when
someone else is around we no longer belong to ourselves, but . . .
I ask you, what is this love, this closeness that can be scared off or
pushed aside by absolutely everything that exists in the world?

As for the macrocosm, one would have to quote the entire
book. The "biotosis" shakes the entire world and everything and
everyone in it. Its nature and its power is to fuse all mankind and
all men's thoughts and feelings, the very ultimate in empathy
and fellow-feeling. Is that not the aim, the dream, of every con-
structive social thinker since thinking began? Perhaps. Is it a
good idea? And if it is, does it matter whether the directing
force is human or something else?

These are the questions the authors confront, and they do it
in many ways: in the idiom of the scientific congress, the cloak-
room argument, the family discussion, but always, always, in
terms of heartbeat and personal pain and the interaction of
thought and technology with the constellations that operate
inside the human skin.

In the last paragraph of the book you will find these words·
"People should know more than what was or will be. People
must know that which must never be."

This is reminiscent of a recent remark of Ray Bradbury s. In a
discussion of *1984*, Bradbury pointed out that the world George
Orwell described has little likelihood of coming about—largely
because Orwell described it. "The function of science fiction is
not only to predict the future," Bradbury said, "but to prevent
it." Consider thoughtfully this Soviet version of that very
thought.

THEODORE STURGEON
San Diego, 1977

World Soul

Love's exchange of glances
Puts out the flame of endless striving.
Let each receive life from the whole
And then return to it anew.

GOETHE, "World Soul"

He is only a voice. A plain human voice recorded on a narrow strip of magnetic tape. That tape is his body. It is very old, and we are very careful with it. That's why it's been kept in an airtight room for the last few centuries.

It's neither cold nor hot, neither dry nor humid in here. A diffuse light penetrates the windows that make up one wall of the room. Beyond the windows lie green fields and a deep dark sky covered with clouds as tall as mountains. The sun slides across the walls, a small yellow moving spot.

He feels night acutely. He dies again every night. But he is full of hope. He knows that morning will come, and the sun will refract into a million parts on the milky walls, and people will come to him. He is here for them.

Excerpts from Sergei Arefyev's
Unwritten Diary

I PRESSED THE BUTTON and the door opened. I entered the room, straining my senses to take everything in.

"All right, all right, yes, that's just what I told him, and I'm not going to go back on my word!"

A man with a mane of hair and round cat eyes was roaring into the videophone, where his interlocutor's lips were flapping silently.

"And if you intend to support him, then you can go to hell too!" he shouted. "Even if you are my friend! That's right, buddy, that's how it is!"

The red face squeaked pathetically and disappeared from the videophone screen. Meanwhile, I had time to observe the luxurious black eyebrows, low forehead, and firm jaw of the research director of the Institute of Telepathy. There was a smell of orthotobacco, grown by the latest bioscientific methods, and his hefty amateur boxer's fists were reflected in the transparent surface of the desk. The director's green eyes transfixed me.

"Ermolov," the man announced, and my hand was briefly squashed in a steel grip. "Sit down, sit down."

I leaned back and felt the cool plastic on my shoulders. It was clear to me what kind of man stood before me, spread-legged and leaning on the desk. He and I wouldn't be able to communicate. We would be talking two different languages. I was disappointed to find that this institute had a director like that—I was expecting someone different.

"Here are your papers," he said, his fat fingers carefully unfastening the clips of the green folder. "By the way, our chief research director is sick. I'm his deputy." He gave me the chief director's name, an Armenian collection of consonants.

So that was it. I was just unlucky. It seemed to be turning into a habit. I was relentlessly lowering myself into the ranks of the failures. It was as though everyone conspired to help me fail in every possible way.

"Your whole life is in here," Ermolov said unexpectedly, scattering photocopies, pieces of film, and reams of paper stamped and sealed by a variety of institutions.

I shuddered. It surprised me that old eyebrows took such an interest in ancient files. Of course those papers did reflect my life. But I had always felt that they did so rather superficially.

"You graduated from boarding school," Ermolov said, setting aside a golden sheet of paper decorated with light-blue pictures of books and rocket ships.

How perceptive! School days, dear old complicated school days. How long ago it all was! From the whirlwind of memories an almost forgotten episode comes back to me.

Even back then I had a special feeling, which followed me throughout my life: a sense of the greatness that fate held in store for me.

As long as I can remember, my life was spent in expectation of grand and earth-shattering events, in which I would have the starring role. There wasn't even a shadow of conceit or vanity in this. It was simple elemental faith, sown in my soul by nature herself.

I knew that I would do something absolutely great, something that would in its scope overwhelm everything that had ever been done by men before me. It would be impossible to measure on the usual human scale. My action would be immeasurably valuable.

Only I did not know when this would happen.

I waited.

Sometimes I wanted to rush things, and I would act. As a rule, this would end badly. Or ridiculously—which was even worse.

When I was ten, I ran away from the school to the Great Preserve. I dreamed of becoming the great tamer of all the animals that were left on earth. My classmates all played at Space or Moon City and collected rare pictures of Jupiter and Saturn, which they wheedled from famous cosmonauts, while I dreamed day and night of commanding armies of tamed tigers and benevolent panthers. My ears quivered with the sound of the brush parting under the weight of the great body of a wild animal, and the words of loyalty and submission, spoken in animal language, which, naturally, I had mastered fluently. Mowgli's fame gave me no rest. It took on cosmic proportions in my eyes. I pictured thousands of elephants falling to their knees when I appeared. I stalked toward them across the emerald grass, covered with myriad dewdrops in the sun, and the wise animals greeted me with low murmurs.

Finally, realizing that there was no hope of stifling my burning desire, I ran away from morning calisthenics, daily lessons, badminton, and Pioneer evenings around the electric campfire. My traveling companion was Zholya, a fair freckled boy with wide-set eyes. Awed by my fantasies, he was ready to follow me to the ends of the earth.

We were lucky. We got to the borders of the preserve, located on the other side of Lake Baikal, in twenty-four hours. The driver of the aerocar landed near the tall white building that stood at the edge of the forest.

"There are the administrative offices of the Great Preserve. That's where you'll find your father."

I nodded, and we climbed down the rope ladder to the soft, damp earth. The driver waved his silver-gloved hand and smiled, and the car slowly rose in the air, leaving us in its exhaust, smelling of oil, paint, and heated metal. We watched him leave, and for a second I felt a nagging stab of loneliness in my chest. We didn't go to the administration building, where neither of us had a father; we hid in the woods. When night fell, we crossed the boundary of the preserve. This was easy, since the barriers were intended for strong and stupid animals, not for two clever and agile boys. We swam across the artificial moat, sneaked through the infrared zone, climbed through the series of wire fences, and found ourselves in a deep virgin forest. Of course, we got lost immediately, but that, after all, was our goal.

I don't remember exactly all my feelings during this adventure. But I will never forget the horror we felt when we heard the cry of an animal in the still of the night. It was right near us, practically at our necks. Under the high protracted howl there was an evil rasping, a burbling, as though the animal were choking on its own anger. We huddled up to an old pine tree that was trembling too, and peered silently into the inky darkness. I felt no desire to meet the roaring animal at all. At that moment, the forest came alive. Every leaf and twig could move, jump, bite. The huge black tree trunks, entwined above us into an invisible whispering canopy, looked like the legs of giants. They kicked us and we bounced about like footballs. They toppled down, pinning us to the damp earth sprinkled with rustling live branches.

We were found the next day by rangers.

In torn clothes, bruised and scratched, and, I think, with muddied tear tracks on our dirty cheeks, we were returned to school.

That night we reported to our pals. In my version, I did not exaggerate the success of our expedition, but I did give a rather colorful account of the forest. I think I mentioned a rhinoceros, a deer, and a rabbit.

Then Zholya took the floor. He was brief:

"We did a dumb thing, and that's that."

Then he added:

"As for all the stuff he told you ... about all that beauty. He was as scared as a rabbit, as timid as a deer, and as stupid as a rhino."

"Then you did well at college," Ermolov said. His irritating voice awakened me from my reverie and shifted my train of thought to another track.

Did well in school? The wrong way of putting it! It wasn't school for me. They didn't teach me, I taught them. I soared higher than the most precocious mathematicians and theoretical physicists. I finished the official four-year course of studies in two years.

"However, you were not permitted to take final exams because of your many attempts to prove the theoretical possibility of perpetual motion."

Ermolov set aside the minutes of my report at the faculty scientific council and looked at me attentively. I had been right from the very start. He had the eyes of an enraged panther. Two saucers of sunflower oil with evil dots in the middle. Why didn't he change their color? That was being done. Navy-blue eyes with a black rim were popular in Europe. Some eccentrics wore purple eyes. They weren't my taste, but they would have been better than those cat eyes.

He stared at me for a minute. What he saw, I couldn't tell. But I stood firm. I was dressed modestly. I wore a leisure suit of light-blue oxopolymer. My chest and back were open to the invisible streams of air conditioning whirling throughout the office. I was sitting confidently and at ease. My face was calm, attentive, slightly strained. I knew, of course, that they didn't like that look. It was too easy to suppose that in your heart you were cursing the interviewer. But I enjoyed sitting with my hypocritical face here in the Institute of Telepathy. Let him guess, the old devil with thick eyebrows, what I thought of him!

Ermolov lowered his gaze and set aside part of the papers.

"So," he said, thumping a paperweight on my file as though putting a heavy marble period to that part of our conversation. "And finally, there is your epic sojourn with the Committee on Inventions."

Epic. I appreciated the ironic condescension he gave the word.

The committee, the committee. All steel, concrete, and glass. Thousands of intense and sleek workers scurrying down the long halls. The inoffensive hum of computers. A seemingly monotonous and soothing job: convert an inventor's proposal into computer language, hand it to the electronic brain to mull over, record its answer, and convey it to the inventor. Nothing spectacular, and most important, no mistakes. The machines remember everything that has ever been done in a given field since before the birth of Christ. They never slip up, and their objectivity is above reproach.

And yet all the time I was there I felt that I was being watched by hundreds, even thousands of human eyes. Dilated eyes, youthful eyes with gleaming whites, dull old eyes with red veins, sly eyes, sultry women's eyes, and the impatient eyes of businessmen. They stared, demanded, implored. Every proposal was a naked human heart. It throbbed and trembled. Look at me, I'm smart, too! I'm original and clever, too! Look at what I've invented! Look at me! No, me! Me!

The flood of inventions carried more than just new ideas and new speculations. It also splashed the foam of violent human conceit into our little skyscraper.

And then one day Eri showed up. His name was a clumsy shortened form of Erik. I later suggested that he abbreviate it to "E." Everyone said that was silly, but no one could explain why.

Eri, like his name, did not make a reassuring impression. Thick black hair, a chronic head cold, and eyeglasses set in frames left over from the War of the Roses. He came into the room, tripped over the perfectly smooth joint in the plastic floor that no one else had ever tripped on, looked around in confusion, and emitted some unintelligible sound. I think it was "Eeehhhh."

He was in luck. I was alone in the office, and so there was no one there to laugh up his sleeve, jump up from his desk with exaggerated politeness and laughter in his eyes, and shower him with unnecessary questions. I waited for the guy to become oriented and then asked:

"Do you want to see me?"

He smiled.

"How would I know? Maybe."

I shook his hand, feeling the flabby touch of his warm palm, and offered him a seat. He handed me a sheet of paper covered with tiny scribbles. It was his proposal.

I read it and realized that I had a genius in front of me.

I might have mumbled, "Amazing."

Eri looked over his glasses with his sunny blue eyes and smiled again. Then I realized that this genius was a child. He needed direction, and I decided to provide it.

Eri's proposal was for a method of synthesizing high polymer compounds from atmospheric gases.

"By the way," Ermolov said, "how did you ever get the job in the committee after the business of the perpetual motor at the university?"

"Accidentally."

My God, of course it was accidental! If I hadn't known Lola . . . and what was our relationship? Nothing more than an accident. Five years ago a slim female form slipped from the diving board into the green depths of the pool, and I was the first one to realize that she was not coming up. Then there were streams of water pouring from her thin Grecian nose—much later came the time of what she called our friendship.

"So," Ermolov said once again, "you and this fellow worked on this unrealizable project which you then brought to a resounding failure."

What did he want from me? I was interested in coming to work here. But did he have to extract my soul? Or was he just leading up to a well-documented rejection? Why didn't he just say so?

Ermolov gathered all my papers. He evened up the pile and smoothed the photocopy lying on top.

"There is enough here for me to give you the most categorical no. The facts are against you. The papers say that you are a habitual dreamer and a stubborn researcher of absurdities."

I stood up. The air in the room had become dry and hot. My throat was dry and my face was flushed. That Ermolov was a typical ape. But how long would I be unemployed? I was damned tired of walking up wide institutional staircases, ringing the bell on doors that said "Chief Research Director," and going down the stairs twenty minutes later. I was fed up with the false faces made by intelligent men who were forced to lie to me and turn me down. I was tempted to give it all up. With my reputation I couldn't pursue science. But I believed in myself—so I kept telling myself.

"Judge for yourself," Ermolov was saying, chopping the air with his hand. "You failed to graduate largely as a result of your own stubbornness. I personally can understand your professors. They couldn't give a degree to someone who preached the possibility of perpetual motion. You quit the committee because work got in the way of your dabbling with Erik Erdman's invention. Your dabbling ended in nothing, and now you're trying to get a job in our institute."

Should I punch him in the face or just walk out? God, what a repulsive character!

"If our Academician"—Ermolov repeated that Armenian name again and I missed it again—"were in my place, then of course he would turn you down. But you're in luck. I am of a different opinion. We need people with original thinking, even if they ride their hobbyhorses."

"And for this, I suppose you expect me to be very grateful?"

"Don't get excited. I'm speaking frankly with you. Telepathy is at a dead end right now. We need to make a qualitative leap. I feel that this can be done only by attracting new blood. Obviously you have not applied here without some idea in the back of your mind. I'd like you to share it with me."

So, they were experiencing a vacuum of ideas right now. Well, the circumstances were good; there was room to move around in. I began to talk in a hoarse nervous voice.

"The energy field created by the brain can be fixed in ways besides biocurrents and shortwave radiation. I have an idea for a concentrator of brain waves, which up to now have not been used either by your telepathic transcorder or by any other devices."

"The waves you speak about—have they been identified?"

"Yes, but...."

"What?"

"There's much work to be done. And too much for one man. That's why I've come to you."

Ermolov stood and plodded across the office. There was something pre-Neanderthal about him. Long arms dangling at his knees, thick bull neck, rolling powerful shoulders. Against the blue light coming through the window he looked like an idol carved in gray stone.

"Yes, work," he said. "You must remember that at all times. Don't dream, don't philosophize—work. Experiments, experiments, and more experiments. Otherwise you and I will part company very quickly. Here's a pass. Go to room 108."

I left the institute late. A gray stillness blanketed the street. Cars flying by whistled through the air. The lights had not been turned on yet, and I walked along a boulevard of blue trees and blue-gray bushes. I was looking for the nearest videophone, to call Erik.

We still hadn't dropped our idea. It was too alluring. In the official form in the space allotted for "Name of invention" we had put the long and dull: "Creation of artificial bioactive enzymatic systems with the aim of a directed and controlled synthesis of polymer compounds from water and atmospheric oxygen and carbon dioxide." But in practice it was both much simpler and much more complex.

Erik was a specialist in biology. He had cultured a piece of living tissue with a marvelous property. Like a plant, it used the oxygen and carbon dioxide in the air, turning them not into regular cellulose and plant proteins, but into long molecules of polymers. Like a plant, it fed on air, water, and a small mixture of mineral salts. As soon as I read Erik's proposal, I immediately went with him to his lab. That was standard procedure for the committee, if the invention or discovery seemed to warrant it. I saw something resembling a fish tank covered with a glass bell. On the surface of the thick deep-green liquid floated an opalescent flower. At least it first seemed like a flower. It was translucent and the color of pale ivory. Its irregular shape had an elusive beauty that captivated the eye, as though movement itself had been frozen for a split second before you. But every few seconds something would happen, and the petals would rise like waves, fall, and run off in different directions, trying to catch each other and never succeeding.

"It's beautiful."

"That's not the point. The point is that it's useful," Erik grumbled.

"That's true."

I smiled and Erik smiled back in understanding.

"Well, what does it do?"

"Inside this flower there is a tissue that exudes polymer as simply as you exhale. The polymer is composed of proteinlike molecules with a high molecular weight. The structure of these molecules is not as complex as that of natural proteins, but it in no way resembles the usual industrial polymers. It contains sulfur, iron, magnesium, and many other elements. However, that is not the important thing. After all, lumber, cotton, leather, and oil are also manufactured by living matter. And they all have high molecular weight, too. However, the properties of these natural polymers cannot be fundamentally altered by man's will. Nature gave them a specific biosynthesis, and nothing else can be expected from them. And that's the way it's been until the development of radiation genetics. My invention pertains to that area of biological study. The living tissue obtained by strong radiation of the seaweed *Opalinariaos medium*—what I call the biotosis—is capable of producing the polymer which formed this strange flower."

"Does it always take this shape?" I asked, fascinated by the yellowish gleam of the biotosis.

"No! That's just it!"

I seemed to have hit upon the whole point of his invention.

"When the hereditary factors are changed, the structure of the polymer molecules is also changed, and you obtain a completely new material, and that means a new form of flower as well. So by regulating the genetic characteristics of the biotosis, which is easy to do with radiation or chemical action, you can control the properties of the polymers. And don't forget that these polymers are obtained from nothing more than air, water, and simple mineral salts!"

I had long hated factories. To me they symbolized man's violence over nature. Once, as a child, I had been flying over the autumn steppe with my father. The air was like the sea, huge and tender, and it carried us and our vehicle easily and freely. Suddenly Father said:

"Look, a factory."

I saw smokestacks with red and gray caps of smoke, black-spotted red walls, gloomy towers, reflections of fire in the windows, complicated twisted tubing, a web of wiring, cars, railroad tracks—as though a disgusting animal of concrete, glass, and steel had lain on the beautiful and joyful earth, an animal that roared and dug up the earth with its claws, raising clouds of poisonous dust. I shared my opinions with Father. He laughed.

"You're wrong. Factories represent man's victory over nature's elemental forces. They are our power and the foundation of our progress. They're not always beautiful, that's true. But what can you do? Is your stomach beautiful, or your liver, or your heart? But you still need them."

Nevertheless, I retained a distaste for the creations of man that made the insulted and raped earth moan and scream.

Listening to Erdman, I pictured chemical factories without machinery, towers, or piping. Just a biotosis lying there and growing. Just go and pick the petals.

"And have you been obtaining much polymer from biotoses like this?" I asked Erik.

Some overly rouged woman at the next desk snickered and quickly turned away. Erik was embarrassed.

"Unfortunately, this is it. The biotosis has stopped growing," he said, spreading his hands.

I understood. That snicker had told me a lot about him. He wasn't overly appreciated by the Committee on Inventions. I felt deep sympathy for Erik.

I suddenly noticed a familiar figure ahead of me. I recognized her as a worker at the Institute of Telepathy and I raced off after her.

"Hello!"

Two blue eyes looked at me with curiosity and a tinge of mockery.

"Oh, it's you."

"I believe we'll be working together?"

"Nearby." She smiled like a child, openly and sincerely rather than for effect.

"Shoulder to shoulder?"

"Maybe."

"Arm in arm, leg in leg, in step?"

Her laugh tinkled like a fallen coin. "I can't walk in step."

"Shall we practice a bit now?" I carefully touched her cool elbow. "You're not Russian. What's your name?"

"No, no." She moved away, a bored expression crossing her face. Then she said: "My name is Ruzhena."

"Czech?"

"Uh-huh."

We walked down the boulevard. The streetlights were on and everything was spoiled; the blue trees and smoky bushes had disappeared.

"Have you been working with Karabichev long?"

"Two years."

"What kind of a man is he, in your opinion? I'm interested in my future boss. Ermolov only introduced us briefly. I didn't even get a good look at him."

I like to ask questions like that. You kill three birds with one stone. You learn about some third person, you learn about the person who answers, and finally, you develop a new relationship.

"He's smart."

"Oh!"

"Handsome."

"Yes?"

"Effective. He invented the XZ Modulator."

"You don't say!"

All three birds escaped unharmed. I hadn't even heard of the XZ Modulator. Better find out.

"And your name is Sergei, no?"

"Ermolov introduced us, you know."

"Oh, I never listen when I'm being introduced. If I look too hard, then I can't hear. I get confused."

"I see. That means I made a spectacular impression on you?"

"Specta—no, no!" That laugh again, like a handful of coins tossed into a crystal vase.

"What kind, then?"

"Funny. You're funny."

She was laughing so hard, it made my skin crawl!

"Do I really look like a clown?"

"Are only clowns funny? A very, very serious person can be a little funny too."

"You mean I'm too serious?"

"Uh-huh." And she laughed again.

We reached the end of the boulevard and came out onto the square full of bustling people and cars.

"Look at the robots coming home from work," I said, pointing at the dark mass moving in the middle of the traffic.

"Yes. I always feel sorry for them somehow."

"Why?"

"You know, I see them early in the morning as they set off. They're so submissive, quiet, and . . . helpless. And funny, with their hooks, and claws, and whiskers. Everything in them is spinning and moving and they're always doing something. And often at the wrong time. At home we have a robot elevator operator. He's so funny! And from my window, I can see a robot traffic controller. He's funny too. And polite."

"You like things to be funny?"

"No, not funny, cute."

"Cute?"

"Yes. I love children. They're so cute."

"Do you have any?"

Ruzhena laughed. That meant she didn't.

"I turn off here," she said.

I waved goodbye, and we parted. Then, trying to remain inconspicuous, I watched her run into the open doors of the aerobus and disappear without looking back.

The videoscreen in the public phone naturally was out of order, and it took me a long time to reach Erik. Finally I heard his voice:

"Is that you, Sergei?"

"Yes. Listen, Eri, I got the job with the telepathists; I've finally anchored myself. We'll be able to run experiments in their labs."

"Marvelous, Sergei, marvelous! My situation is still the same."

"I understand."

We said goodbye.

I didn't feel like going home. My father was there, and he could spoil my mood for the entire evening. How about the reading room? I had a headache. I decided to go to Lola's.

I got home late. Father was still up, sitting in his room, smoking and looking out the window with the kind dreamy eyes of a drunken giant. I never knew my mother; she had died a long time before. I was brought up, or rather, almost not brought up at all, by my father.

"Where were you?"

"At Lola's."

"Oh." Clouds of smoke poured from his mouth and dissolved in the corrugated walls. "How are things with them?"

"Going downhill. They're becoming automated consumers and TV addicts. Disgusting to watch it happen."

"My son. . . ."

Lecture coming up. Begging exhaustion, I sought haven in my room.

I lay on my bed, unable to sleep. On the opposite wall was a photo of Lola, three-quarter view, and reflections of the streetlights glided along it. For some reason I kept hearing Ruzhena's bell-like voice saying "Sergei."

The next day I was examining the results on the biotosis taken by the latest devices when Karabichev came over.

"Listen, Arefyev, drop your squiggles for a while."

"All right, why?"

"One of our people is giving an interesting lecture. Revolutionary ideas. New prospects. More accurately, putting an end to all prospects in telepathy. Go have a look."

I barely squeezed into the crowded auditorium. A tall young man in glasses stood on the stage and ticked off his conclusions in a strident falsetto.

"Our research has confirmed our theories. Human sensations, the conscious and the subconscious—in other words, that which we call the state of the mind—are manifested in a system of impulses distributed in the cortex and the subcortex of the brain. Every individual has a specific arrangement of impulses, or as we term it, a characteristic code of impulses. It is related to the physical and chemical properties of the organism and is its natural characteristic. This system of registering sensations is just as uniquely individual as, say, fingerprints. In telepathic contact the acceptor's code is violated by the insurgence of the donor's impulses into the subcortex, which is accompanied by serious nervous disorder, and even occasionally by temporary insanity. A safe outcome of telepathic communication can only occur in the case of total identity of the impulse codes of the donor and the acceptor. But that is impossible. Among all the people on earth there are no two people with the same mind code. All people are antipathetic telepathically. There are no sympathetic people. In short, we are repeating the business of the foreign protein. We know that a living organism will not accept all the proteins of another. In just this way the mind of a person will struggle against the mind of another person trying to penetrate it. This struggle is intense and so dangerous that it sheds doubt on the very possibility of telepathic contact between people. We, of course, will not cease our attempts, but the difficulties that stand in our path are formidable, and we must keep that in mind."

After the speaker came a professor I did not know. He tossed back his gray hair and said:

"Eh. . . ." Then he stopped.

"Hhhhmmm," he said after a few seconds. "Our young colleague has cited many interesting facts that demand attention. But youth, as you know, tends to be rather categorical and, as you know, tends to jump to unsubstantiated conclusions. I would like to keep you from jumping to a hasty conclusion. It cannot be that the problem to which we have devoted our lives has reached a dead end and that that is the end to it all. Of course, there are difficulties and there will be others, but the end, of course, is in sight, and it, so to speak, must be found."

I left. Behind me resounded applause, shouts, and chairs scraping against the floor.

There was a spontaneous meeting in the lab. Karabichev gave a fiery talk denouncing the speaker and emphasizing the great meaning of telepathy for the future of mankind. It was like a pep talk.

"Is the work new? The newest. Is it hard? You bet. Can we drop it because of some theoretical dead end? Never! Will we beat our heads against the wall until we break through? We will! Of course we will!"

Then Ermolov showed up and sent everyone back to his post.

"Back to work! Everyone, back to work. The experiments will show us the way out. We have to run experiments, hundreds of thousands of them, and then everything will become clear. First we must examine the nature of the phenomenon, and then we can yap about sympathies and antipathies."

After Ermolov left, Karabichev came up to me.

"Ermolov told me that you have an idea for concentrating the energy given off by the brain. What do you have in mind?"

"A new approach. I'm not much interested in telepathic perturbations. I feel it's more important to capture bioenergetic radiation. And to concentrate it into a parallel beam. We may even come up with a new industrial source of energy. I hope that it will be qualitatively different from all known radiation."

"Do you have an apparatus?"

"No, but...." I made a vague gesture to imply that such an apparatus could be constructed.

"Well, you have my support. For now, get to know the people and the routine here. In a week or so, give me your proposal, your application for equipment, and get to work. Let me know if you need help."

I looked into Ruzhena's room. It was a kingdom of cleanliness and the latest electronics. Squiggly colored lines lit up and disappeared on oscilloscopes. Ruzhena, in her white coat, with her rosy cheeks and blue eyes like a good fairy out of a Scandinavian fairy tale, walked among the counters. Once in a while she wrote something down or turned something off. She worked confidently, casually, almost gracefully. In school, when I was very little, I had been in love with a girl like her. I still have a memory of the marvelous rosy blue cloud that enveloped me whenever I saw her.

"Oh, it's you Sergei!" She smiled at me as if I were an old friend.

"Go on working; don't let me disturb you."

"You do disturb me. You embarrass me." She laughed.

"All right, I'll leave. Listen, Ruzhena, shall we walk home together?"

She looked at me a little longer than usual. Then she nodded conspiratorially.

"Yes."

But Ruzhena and I did not get to take our walk. Erik called
in the afternoon.

"Come over to the committee today. I have news."

"What's up?"

"Come over, I'll tell you."

"At least give me a hint."

"The biotosis grew."

I gathered up my papers and went over to Erik's without
waiting for the work day to end. I was so excited that I missed
my stop. The news was astounding. We had struggled with that
little chunk of watery material for two years. But our results up
until now had been pitiful. The biotosis would grow to the size
of a tulip and then its development would stop. The ratio of the
formed polymer to the amount of living tissue was too small. It
was ridiculous to talk about industrial applications for now. It
was like raising apples and using only the skins. I once asked
Erik:

"Wouldn't it be easier to determine the chemical reactions
and then repeat them *in vitrio?*"

"Try to figure it out," Erik smiled sourly.

He was right. We could spend our entire lives studying the
mechanisms of the reaction. And we didn't have the time.
Science in our day was impatient.

Powerful waves of scientific achievements had crashed down
on people, devouring the traditional concepts of space and time,
of gravity and the creation of the earth, of nature and the properties of living organisms. It was painful in times like these to
be fooling with the biotosis when it seemed so hopeless. Success
would come if we could learn to churn out tons and tons of
polymer. Meanwhile all we had on hand was about fifty grams
of a yellowish mass in the shape of a weird flower. Sometimes I
just wanted to drop the whole thing and take up something
simple and clear-cut, but it was too late to turn our backs on the
biotosis.

Work on the biotosis had been turned down by Erik's lab a
long time ago, on the grounds that it would lead nowhere. We
had to run experiments at night, when no one disturbed us.

"How did you do it?" I began as I burst into Erik's office.
He was sitting down, having a quiet smoke.

Nobody came across as more of a do-nothing than Erik. As long as I'd known him, he'd been sitting and smoking. He thought a lot, but there was no way of telling about what. His bosses didn't think very highly of him. Bosses like to see workers with anxious faces bustling around new equipment. Lots of points, lots of lines on a graph, proof positive that you're doing research.

"Gathering thousands of points and plotting curves, collecting variables, is something that creative abortions can do," Erik would say adjusting his prehistoric eyeglasses. "All you need is one point, one curve—the most important one. We need invention, not research; synthesis, not analysis."

He had a minimax program: a minimum of analysis, and a maximum of synthesis.

I had the feeling that Erik was always climbing out of his own skin. He was always striving higher, and that striving brought us closer together. I also wanted to raise myself up by my own bootstraps.

"The hell of it all is that I don't know and can't understand how it happened," Erik said.

"What did you do to it?"

"Nothing. It's right where it always was. Look for yourself."

I looked. The biotosis had quintupled in size. Now a flower about sixteen inches in diameter was floating in the tank. Its color had changed somewhat and there were pale pink streaks on its petals.

"But how?"

"That's what I'm wondering. Yesterday it was the same as usual. This morning, when I came in to work, I didn't see anything different either. I didn't touch it or do anything with it. Just before the seminar I moved the tank from the table to the top shelf; Nikolai Nikolayevich needed the table. After the seminar I went to lunch, and when I got back and started to put the tank back I saw that the biotosis had grown. I called you. That's it."

I looked at the table and at the shelf. The tank had traveled approximately thirty inches. The biotosis had been raised and lowered, and it had grown. It didn't make any sense.

"What a pain!" Erik laughed. "What can you do with it? It's a mystery."

"You don't have anything radioactive around here, do you?" I asked.

"Don't be silly! Just test tubes."

"I don't get it."

"May I?" Nikolai Nikolayevich's lab assistant came in. His name was Oleg or Igor, I couldn't remember which.

"Erik, we forgot a demonstration exhibit. Nikolai Nikolaye-vich just conducted it," he said.

"Yes, here it is," Erik said, handing him a jar with a preserved frog head in it.

He took it, looked at us, and smiled.

"Still enjoying your red flower? It's so pretty the way it glows!"

"What makes you say it glows?" Erik was surprised. "It doesn't glow."

The fellow looked into the tank.

"That's strange, it isn't glowing now." He shook his head. "It did at the seminar. And how!"

We perked up.

"Did you see it, Erik?" I asked.

"No, I was sitting with my back to it."

"And what did you see, Igor?"

"Oleg."

"Sorry, Oleg."

"I remember it perfectly. The flower glowed as if it had a lightbulb in it. It was very crowded at the seminar—I guess there were about forty people stuffed into this room, nowhere to sit—so I climbed up here. I could look down into the tank at your flower. It was just level with Nikolai Nikolayevich's head. I noticed that it was glowing and changing color. I even thought to myself, what a pretty flower the guys have grown, they shouldn't knock them so much—"

"Thanks. Did you happen to notice what was happening to the flower? It glowed and that's it? It wasn't growing too, was it? Moving?"

"Nope. Just glowing, as far as I could see. And to tell the truth, I wasn't paying that much attention. Nikolai Nikolayevich was telling really interesting stuff about his experiments."

"All right. Well, thanks, Igor," Erik said.

"Oleg."

"Sorry, Oleg. You gave us some very interesting information. Thanks!"

"Maybe it was Nikolai Nikolayevich's exhibits?" I began uncertainly after Oleg had left.

"Just a minute." Erik jumped up and ran out of the room. He came back ten minutes later with a pile of jars, tubes, and boxes.

"This is the lot!" he sighed. Like madmen we picked up exhibit after exhibit and held it up to the biotosis. No effect. Then we piled them all up by the tank and stared at the damn flower. No glow, no movement.

"The hell with it!" shouted Erik. "Let's get out of here. We need to think, think, and think some more."

We went for a walk. We wandered around Moscow in silence.

"It's pleasant to find yourself on a street where you've never been before. Then you become a stranger to yourself," said Erik.

"Only if the street doesn't look like any that you have been on. Listen, Erik, let's go visit a good friend of mine. She invited me over tonight anyway."

About a month later I talked to Erik by videophone.

"Well, how are things?"

"I've been subjecting it to all sorts of rays. I used ultraviolet, infrared, X-ray, alpha, beta, and gamma rays, radio waves along the whole spectrum, and so on."

"And?"

"No change, and when I handled it too roughly, it wilted." Erik's face was long and sad.

"All right, don't be depressed, we'll figure something out. Are you still seeing Lola?"

He nodded.

"Give her my regards."

"You sound awfully cheerful. How are things with you?"

"Moving along. I'll drop by and fill you in."

Of course, my cheerfulness had nothing to do with my work, even though it would have been a sin to complain about it now. The concentrator for brain energy was nearly ready. Its chrome surfaces gleamed, beckoning to the researcher. There were a few things missing, but in a week's time, controlled experimentation could begin. I doubted that it would work just the way we wanted it to. But we had to begin somewhere. And I was sure that the concentrator would bring me grief rather than pleasure.

It was Ruzhena who raised me to such heights. When I walked around Moscow with her, down ancient streets populated by smug cats and pensioners bent over by old age, I felt that I was walking with a person I'd known for years, down to the last hair on her head. And yet every time she was unexpectedly new and fresh for me, even alien.

"I loved you even before you were born, before your parents were born. I loved you when the word 'passion' was not yet known, and people frolicked like children. I loved you before the earth knew men. I loved you always, my love is age-old—"

"Such an old feeling must surely have died by now," Ruzhena laughed.

"Never!" I shouted and we ran down the echoing streets toward Bolshoi Park.

"Listen, Ruzhena," I said as we sat down on a bench in a secluded lane in the park, where it smelled of dampness, and we could hear music and see thousands of lights hidden in the thick foliage.

"Listen, Ruzhena," I said, and she laid her head on my hand and I could feel her silky hair and the warmth of her skin, and I could smell the wonderful perfume that tickled my nostrils like a fresh spring breeze.

"Listen, Ruzhena," I said. "I think that I am a very bad person."

"Oh, that's quite possible," the girl answered. "But that has no bearing on the present situation."

"You see, I keep thinking all the time."

"Don't you get tired?"

"Even when I'm kissing you, I'm thinking."

"That's a cardinal sin."

"Yes. I don't understand why I feel good and why I feel bad. Now here I am, a so-and-so, in a word, bad. But I don't even want to be a good man. Not in the least! I want to remain bad but to feel good. And I certainly don't understand why I feel good with you. You don't do a thing to impress me or to make me like you. Absolutely nothing. And yet I feel good, very good. That's never happened before. What is it?"

"I don't know. I only know when I'm happy and when I'm not. But why? I don't know," Ruzhena answered softly.

Women don't like to analyze certain aspects of life, but I stubbornly pressed on.

"What's the point then? Sometimes it seems to me that we'll never be able to escape our own skins. Man's thought is boundless, but his feelings are enclosed and limited. Man is doomed to live inside his own body to the end of his days. And never—do you understand, never—will he know another organism the way he senses himself. Logical unity, ideological community, commodity exchange—all this is important, necessary, and right. Without it man would not have become man. But—"

"But limited to that he will never become superman?" Ruzhena asked. Her eyes grew darker, more serious.

"Yes. That's it exactly. Man is trapped physically and materially. No verbal agreement can guarantee spiritual agreement. People search for each other all their lives, but this one doesn't suit that one because of work, that one doesn't complement the other's personality, and so on. People are driven by an unquenchable thirst for unity, both physical and moral. People establish clubs, circles, lodges, parties, enter into marriages, take lovers, organize gangs, armies, and countries. Doesn't it seem to you that an unheard scream hovers over human society: *I seek another!?*"

"You're mixed up, Sergei."

"Fine. So be it. But I honestly care about tying up the loose ends."

"What do you want?"

"Everybody asks me that. What can I answer? I can't for now. Time will show what I want. Now I'm just dissatisfied. With myself and with others, too."

"But I hope—"

"Oh, of course, I don't mean you."

We sat in silence and the delicious relaxation left my body. Thoughts drilled screechingly into my skull.

"Sergei, I've been meaning to ask you. . . ."

"What?"

"Why did you leave the Committee on Inventions?"

"Because I wanted to do my own inventing. Erik's biotosis awakened my creative urge. I thought that our work would go quickly, but as you see. . . . By the way, I have a segment of the biotosis with me. I was over at Erik's and I grabbed a piece to run some tests at the institute."

"Let's see."

I took a small flat vial with an open top from my briefcase. A tiny piece of the biotosis floated on the liquid. Ruzhena looked at it with interest.

"It's not growing?"

"No."

Ruzhena laughed.

"What is it?"

"When you said no, you made such a face—like a little boy who didn't get his candy."

"Nonsense. I'd like to see your face after so many failures!"

"Oh, don't be mad. Why don't we go see a good pantomime act. There's one at the Naklonny Theater."

Walking down the paths of the park we saw couples sitting on benches, arms entwined, heads inclined toward each other— silent poses symbolizing trust and sincerity.

"You're very wrong. I'm amazed at you," Ruzhena said. "There's your unity—physical, moral, whatever you want."

She gestured in the direction of the dark paths. I smiled. Ruzhena got mad.

"What about ideas? Doesn't thought unite people, bind them closer together than chains? Hasn't our political system united billions of people?"

"You're right," I said. "You're right. I value and understand the power of love, the energy of work, the depth of blood ties, and so on. But I seek something different in nature. Different! Something else! Goddamn it, something else entirely!"

"What do you want then?"

"Here's what."

I ran up the slope leading to the Moscow River. All the bridges visible from there were lit up, and under them, like black oil slicks, barges with marker lights fore and aft slowly made their way in the dark water. The city lay beyond the river, a heap of jewels.

"There's what I want! There are people there! And there! And over there! And there! No two look alike, they're all different, and yet alike. But each of them is alone physically. Each one is a sealed vessel. I want to unite all of them physically. So that they can feel each other all the time. Do you understand, physically?"

"What for?" Ruzhena's eyes sparkled and laughed.

Of course, a man is not alone if he can look into eyes like those. Of course, a man is happy if eyes like that look at him. Of course, he will bend over and kiss each one separately and then will try to kiss them both at the same time, and of course, fail, and feel silly.

But these are all the sweet familiar tricks of nature—not true unity, just a clever ruse, a game, smoke. You can give in to the game, but how do you hold on to it? The fog lifts, and you're left all alone again.

"It's hard to explain, but I must try. I feel a need for community. Other people don't feel it the same way. There are things I understand, but you don't. There are things you know, but I don't. And there are so many other examples. The thirst for new knowledge and the impossibility of assimilating it alone —and envy and lack of confidence in your own powers. I want to feel all of life, the way it is everywhere, and to guess what the future will be like. And also . . . well, there's so much more."

Ruzhena listened in silence, thoughtful, relaxed, slightly sad.

"People should be brought together even closer," I say.

"How can you feel that they're held together only loosely? There's radio, TV, newspapers, magazines, books, contact at work, contact at home—there are people everywhere. Just people and more people. You can get tired of them all."

"We need a completely new form of communication."

"Telepathy?"

"Antipathy and sympathy. . . . No, that's not it. What would be the point if I crawled into your soul? I want to be with all people, with everybody at the same time."

"But Sergei, that's crazy! How do you know that it's right?"

'If only I did know! That's the problem, I don't know. But I feel a constant agitation. The society in which I live is not at fault, the people who live around me are not at fault. Although much depends on them. I'm not at fault either. It's the voice of evolution. Don't stop. Don't settle. Always be unsatisfied."

"Here we are."

We really were there. We immediately immersed ourselves in the semidarkness that already contained hundreds of invisible, hotly breathing spectators. We found two free seats with difficulty. We lowered our seats. The movement of the mimes was being projected in larger scale onto the ceiling.

Some forty minutes passed. Suddenly I became aware of something wrong. The briefcase on my lap seemed unusually heavy.

"Ruzhena, is that you?" I whispered.

"What?"

There was a resounding crack and snap. Something was tearing off the lock on my briefcase. Frightened and worried, I jumped up.

"Ruzhena, let's go!"

We raced to the exit, tripping over angry feet. In the light I discovered that my case was bulging monstrously and had cracked in several places. When I opened it, pink tongues climbed out of it and dangled helplessly. They burned with a cold ruby light for about thirty seconds and then went out.

"The biotosis!"

"It's grown again. Why?"

It had grown again in some wild inexplicable way. It had grown to make us feel stupid again. It was laughing at us.

"Why is it that you grow when no one asks you, and don't budge when we beg you?" Erik asked angrily, circling the table on which lay a wilted lump of the biotosis. Ruzhena was there too, in a deep armchair, smiling slightly, as usual. Erik and I were experiencing a powerful surge of the hatred that the ignorant have for the mysterious. Nature herself lay before us, multifaceted and elusive. We couldn't cram her tricks into our limited brains and we were angry with her, with ourselves, and with the whole world.

"Maybe it develops periodically?" Ruzhena offered.

"Some periods! One lasted two years, and the other a few weeks."

I got an interesting idea.

"Listen, Erik. You notice the biotosis grows in places where there are a lot of people."

Erik stopped in his tracks.

"An increase in carbon-dioxide concentrations? Heat?" he asked, watching me closely, as though I had just uttered an unspeakable heresy.

"I don't know . . . maybe that's not all. Maybe something else as well."

"We'll test it out."

We didn't say anything else.

The plan of action was clear, so Ruzhena and I left.

"Did you like Erik?"

A giggle. Why did she laugh all the time?

"What's so funny?"

"It's hard to judge on first impressions."

"But nevertheless?"

"I think he's a real scientist."

"What do you mean?"

"He knows how to look and think without distractions."

But I had stopped listening to Ruzhena. A strange feeling resembling jealousy awakened in me. I was listening to it.

"What are you thinking about?" she asked, turning to face me.

"You know, I just imagined that we'd already learned to grow polymer from the air! Buy suits made of biopolymers, build houses out of bioconcrete, and so on. And we'll be depressed. The riddle will be solved, the mystery revealed. Is that it? What should we do? Where will we go?"

"Sergei!" Ruzhena scolded. "A mere hour ago you were happy! Love can't take such crazy turnabouts."

"I was happy, but. . . . Love, loving, it's all nonsense, Ruzhena. Love is closeness, deep and eternal. Nobody's ever known it. Adam and Eve, Romeo and Juliet—a beautiful lie that managed to crawl into the twentieth century. And what it was they really had nobody knows. But for us . . . for us it's all complicated. When we are silent we understand many things. We are part of each other. But as soon as we utter a single word, we create a thought, and it separates us. Do you understand? The thought becomes a third person. It may not be superfluous, but it is the third. And sometimes it *is* superfluous. We don't feel each other, don't see ourselves, we only see it—the thought. Do you understand? I'm not talking about a real third person, like Erik or Karabichev. When someone else is around we no longer belong to ourselves, but ... I ask you, what is this love, this closeness that can be scared off or pushed aside by absolutely everything that exists in the world?"

Ruzhena frowned, and her nostrils flared derisively.

"What nonsense! How can you turn things around so! Sometimes I think that in your eyes the world is upside down. If a feeling exists it's hidden away in the depths of the soul and appears only when it's needed. It functions like a pleasant background against which the picture of a man's life can unfold. It serves as a foundation for the rest of man's feelings. Why are you trying to break down an open door?"

"It's not working, Ruzhena. I keep thinking I'm not doing anything real."

"Just tell me the truth for once. Are you happy with me?"

"It's not working, Ruzhena. Sometimes it's harder for me to be with you than with anyone else. I suspect a hoax."

Ruzhena turned to me. She paled. Her eyes stood out against her gray face, like stars through a cloud. And I felt that any second a wave would knock me down and carry me off, dashing me against rocks and steep shores.

There exists an amazing moment in premonitions. Just before acting, when his peace of mind has disappeared and the event has not yet occurred, a person becomes clairvoyant. This strange moment lasts less than a millionth of a second. It doesn't come to everyone and not always to anyone, but it does come. And then the person knows for sure what will happen and how it will turn out. He knows it before anything has happened. But he also knows that he is powerless to change any of it. He is carried by a wave, the heavy powerful wave of necessity. And he is just a twig in the wave.

"I'm afraid of delusion more than anything else in the world.

Don't you feel that our relationship . . . is also false? We've just agreed to act in a way that keeps things pleasant for us, and we call it love?"

Ruzhena said nothing, and her gray face disappeared in the evening dusk. I felt as though the girl had dissolved in the dusky air and I was alone. I grabbed her shoulder. It was limp.

"Love is the death of loneliness. And with you there are times when I feel unbelievably, inhumanly alone. Not always, no, not always, but nevertheless it happens to me. As soon as I think that I can delude myself and then someone else, I find irrefutable evidence of a con job. Ruzhena, please understand me. I hate falsehood. It may not be so, but the thought that I'm lying to you and to myself sometimes drives me crazy."

"I thought that you were merely funny. But it turns out that you can be frightening. Thank you. I've learned my lesson. And now *I* have some thinking to do. . . ."

I felt the touch of her warm lips on my forehead. As she left, her oblique shadow slowly slipped after her along the pavement. It got shorter and shorter, dissolved, and disappeared with the figure.

I was alone. It always ended this way. I was always left alone. At home, at work, in love. All I had to do was say one sincere word, and they all went running. What were they afraid of? What were words? Action was what counted. Action. The only man worthy of life and freedom was the one who went to fight for them every day. He alone was right. And I wasn't. He fought and I didn't. Only he was worthy. . . . But where was the battle? Whom should I fight? Myself?

Chapter 1

THE AEROBUS, clumsy and heavy, tore out of the rain into fair weather, where it smelled strongly of ozone and the thick steppe grasses shone as if they had been oiled. Low hills appeared in the distance and quickly came closer. The sun fractured itself on the slopes, torn apart by the rain and wind, and gave off blinding orange gleams.

"Looks like we're almost there" said Erik.

Sergei said nothing. They were hunched up in the baggage compartment. They rode among the crates with the biotosis, the equipment, a prefab aluminum hut, and a pile of other things that Karabichev had said might come in handy when he was seeing them off.

The aerobus made a U-turn and softly landed on the damp earth next to a small house that was fenced in by thin metal reeds.

"We're here," the driver announced, opening the doors.

Erik jumped out. The thick ursine scent of the steppe hit him in the face. The air shocked his lungs and blood, and sent waves of energy throughout his body.

"Hey, Sergei, I like it here! The biotosis will flourish out here."

"What?" Sergei's muffled voice came from the back of the bus.

"Great out here," Erik said. "Let's get unpacked!"

"All right." Sergei backed out of the truck, carefully set the crate with the equipment on the ground, and straightened slowly. He was tall and thin and squinted as he looked up.

"The sun is square here," he suddenly said.

Erik looked at the sun.

"All right, let's go to the biostation."

A girl with watermelon cheeks greeted them at the house.

"I'm leaving on your bus," she said. "You're the lords of all you survey."

"Are you a scientist?" Sergei asked.

"Yes, the last of our group."

"How was it out here?"

"Not bad."

"Weren't you bored? Just steppe as far as the eye can see?"

"It was all right."

"No more questions," Sergei grumbled and busily set himself to unpacking.

The girl went out to the truck, dragging two heavy suitcases. Sergei watched her flat square back, which looked like a slab of steel, for some time and then snorted:

"Scientist! 'Lords!' . . . she's a fossil!"

Erik went out of the house and down to the quarry. The huge excavation made long ago was now overgrown with trees and grasses. Long abandoned, it had become a haven for the steppe birds and insects, who made homes for themselves in the myriad holes and burrows in the quarry's slopes. Recently it had been discovered that the clay at the bottom of the pit was unusually fertile. A team of agrobiologists came out, set up the house, and planted the silvery-black Venus seaweed in the pit. But researchers would still be returning for a month or two to run some elaborate experiment or other.

Erik kicked a lump of dried clay lying on the edge of the pit. The lump bounced like a ball, merrily turned over in the air, and skipped down noisily, getting caught in the bushes and luring pebbles and dust after it. It reached the lazy stream at the bottom of the pit in the shape of a huge gray cloud, which, when it fell into the water, shed splashes and showers of light.

"We're like that," said Sergei behind him. "Someone or even some thing gives us a push, and we roll on, taking others with us, until we end up in the nearest puddle."

Erik said nothing in reply. He smiled.

"I think that this is going to be an excellent place for the biotosis," he said after a while.

"Where does the stream come from?"

"I don't know. I was told that it dries up. But the summer is rainy."

"We'll really have a lot of work out here, Eri?"

"Yes. But of course, nobody made us blow our vacation on an attempt to grow the biotosis."

They watched the wind make ash-gray waves in the grass. Erik was thinking about all the work they had in the month ahead. The most important was to discover the optimum growing conditions for the biotosis. They had found the key; all they had to do was turn it in the lock. They had to grow several tons of biopolymer, and then they could talk to their adversaries. The biotosis had taken firm hold of Erik's spirit. He daydreamed about its translucent petals. Lately the flower had begun giving off a delicate scent. Erik could inhale the refreshing and yet heady perfume by the hour.

Sergei, sitting next to him and lazily watching the purple shadows on the quarry floor, wasn't thinking about the biotosis. He was remembering.

The day before yesterday he had run into Karabichev in front of the Mars Cinema. Sergei was standing under the marquee and smoking his eleventh cigarette, waiting for Ruzhena. During the last two months their relationship had become dangerously unsteady. They argued on every date, though they immediately

made up. They laughed less and cried more. They knew the end
was near. The feeling was escaping, like life from a wounded
body; the feeling was leaving just as senselessly and unexpectedly
as it had once come, and they did not know what to do to make
it stay. Sergei stood there, smoking and thinking about Ruzhena,
and he knew that she would not come. She was tired and she
could not take much more of this.

And suddenly he saw Karabichev. Cool, calm, and handsome,
he strode through the excited pleasure-seeking throng. Sergei
thought, There's someone who's happy. At least everything is
clear for him. And on impulse, he called out to him. They stood
in silence because there was nothing to talk about. Karabichev
said, "My mother died." Sergei looked at him. Karabichev was
gazing over the heads of the crowd to where the garlands of
lights formed a carousel. Sergei heard a scream. A man was
shouting piercingly, but his voice carried over the city and no
one heard him. People were going to and fro, exchanging pleas-
antries and telling jokes; shoes scraped against the rough pavement; thin heels tripped a coquettish tattoo; cigarette ashes fell
down like gray snowflakes ... and the scream flew over the city
unheard.

There it is, loneliness, thought Sergei. The loneliness of grief.
I know how alone you are, friend. You can lie to anyone but me.
I hear your scream, I see the invisible tears on your cheeks. Your
hands are clutching the air, squeezing, trying to grasp what is
irretrievably lost.

I sympathize, I understand your sorrow.

I would like to help you, feel your pain. But how?

There isn't a drop of blood in your face. Your dry eyes seem
glassily calm.

Your pain is unique and terrible. You are suffering your loss
and you are waiting for something, anything.

I sympathize, I understand.

No, definitely not. Don't believe me, friend, I don't understand. I hear, I see, but I don't understand. For me to understand you, I must become you, but nature has been building a
barrier between us since time immemorial. No one has ever
crossed it.

And so your pain is not yet my pain. Yes, I hear the scream coming from your mouth, but I can only guess at your feelings.

Your pain is in your heart, your muscles, in every breath you take.

But I first get it through my brain. First and foremost in the brain. It comes to me with words, colors, smells, and the sound of your voice.

I'm disturbed, I'm touched. But what is my disturbance next to your pain!

Yes, your pain is not mine and it never will be my pain. . . .

Sergei invited Karabichev home with him. Karabichev saw the heap of suitcases, knapsacks, and boxes in Sergei's room and learned of their plans to spend their vacation at the Khokai-Rokh Biostation. He listened attentively to Sergei's story of the biolosis and gave him some useful advice. "You have to anticipate everything," he said and in ten minutes had come up with a list of things that would come in handy. He criticized the equipment Erik had picked out and the utensils that Sergei had gotten. Karabichev suggested things that were more compact and cheaper. Sergei accomplished more with him in one evening than he had with Erik in a week. "I'll drop in on you there to see how your invention is going," Karabichev said. Sergei felt that Karabichev liked their idea. For a short time, at least, he was distracted from his grief.

"Let's go," Erik said. "We have to unpack." Sergei stood up, stretched, and gave a farewell glance at the quarry. The sun had begun its trip down to the horizon, and it was dark and gloomy below. The curly green bushes were melting into the pit's dark shadows and the stream had disappeared. Sergei followed Erik to the house.

They unpacked the crates and set up the equipment and furniture. The aluminum hut suggested by Karabichev gave them the most trouble. It had to be assembled, and Erik struggled with it for a long time, adjusting his glasses and wheezing, until he had gotten it right. By late evening everything was finished. There was no room to move inside the biostation itself: the floor was covered with scraps of packing paper, ropes, wire, tapes, and nails. Huge packing crates were piled in the yard. The new aluminum hut with the gamma ray inside was settled on the grass. The equipment was set up and ready for work.

"We'll pick up the garbage in the morning," Sergei said, and both of them collapsed into their beds as if on command.

The next day, Erik, fresh, well rested, and with red pillow marks on his cheek, evaluated the situation:

"So we wish to obtain this polymer in significant quantities. How can we achieve this? First of all we must keep in mind all the peculiarities of the biotosis that we have established. It grows in the presence of large numbers of human beings. Why? Is it the effect of a high level of carbon dioxide? No, we proved it not to be that. We have grown our biotosis in movie theaters, in the subway, at meetings, and at dances."

"Which involved a certain difficulty," noted Sergei, lying half-dressed on the damp and sun-warmed grass. "Remember the time the box with the biotosis burst at Maurizio Colli's concert? It sounded like a bomb exploding. The poor singer blanched and laid his own bomb. We were almost arrested."

Erik thoughtfully began to clean his glasses. "Yes, but let's stick to the subject. We have noted that when it reaches a certain size, the biotosis begins to grow on its own. Very slowly. Very, very slowly. But it does grow. And in that stage all it requires is air, light, and room. I think we should place the samples at the top of the stream in nets. The water is fresh and runs swiftly. We'll be able to add minerals to the water in any concentration we think necessary, and then—"

"I understand! To work, Cicero, to work!" Sergei jumped up. "Let our labor show the world just what we and our biotosis are capable of!"

Thus began a series of amazingly monotonous days, each like a frame in a film hand-cranked through a projector: a man takes a step and keeps taking it and never seems to go anywhere.

First they cleared the bottom of the pit by the stream, removing orange clay soil, and cut back the thick bushes that blocked the way to the source of the stream. Then they cleared the stream of grasses, the thick, gooey silt that was slowing its current, and broken branches and litter. The mud dried and turned into gray pyramids along the banks. The wind blew dust from them and carried it throughout the quarry, powdering the grass with its gray fallout, and only the frequent rains kept the grass fresh and shiny.

It took several days to haul down the boxes with the biotosis, unpack them, and carefully suspend the pale-pink masses in nets in the stream. There were twelve crates and plenty of work with each one, so that it was not till a week later that the trembling nets were stretched over the stream, each covered with cloth to protect the biotosis from direct sunlight.

At the source of the stream they placed a bio-ionite nozzle that fed "vitamins" to the biotosis. That required hauling more crates, this time the ones with the adsorbents, to the stream's source. They carried over two tons of ionites across the uneven quarry floor and along its crumbly slopes. It was tedious work. They took samples of the water at various depths and then analyzed them on the spectrograph. To avoid climbing up to the lab with every sample, Erik brought the apparatus down to the stream. He set up a tent and worked in it some twelve hours a day. Snuffling, adjusting his glasses, dropping the samples, and tripping over his own feet, he still managed to do five hundred analyses a day.

"The hell with it!" Sergei said one day. "I want to have a good meal, and I don't give a damn anymore about this biotosis. Let's go up."

They went up to the station, shaved, bathed, took an electro-shower, making their bodies tingle and glow, changed into fresh underwear, and got out a bottle of Aso, a thick, rich liqueur. Sergei opened several cans, emptied them into the heater, and three minutes later they were eating with enormous gusto.

"By the way, I keep forgetting to ask," Erik said. "What's the status of your mind concentrator?"

"Nil. It's not concentrating a thing. But there's always a silver lining. It senses weak biocurrents at a distance of three to six feet. That's very handy. Ermolov liked it, even praised it. Now people won't have to be wired up with that whole slew of receptors and transmitters. Instead they'll place my apparatus next to the person and record the session. That's it. Clean and simple."

Erik laughed and shook his head.

"What an achievement."

"No, listen. My concentrator turned out to be useful for another purpose. Do you know what's involved in long-distance control of free-moving automatons? The automation guys have been breaking their heads on this one. It's hellishly complicated. The command has to be coded, then sent to the robot in the form of a radio signal. The programming subassembly is a complex, clumsy, and inaccurate mechanism. Translating a thought or desire into a signal for an automaton is a difficult task that becomes simple with the help of my machine. The biocurrents of the programmer are easily sensed by the concentrator, which is mounted into the receiving device of the automaton. See how easy?"

"Sergei, why did you go work at the Institute of Telepathy, really?"

"God only knows, but I somehow thought that telepathy was today's most urgent problem. It probably is. Mutual understanding—that's what's lacking. People should understand each other completely. But when I saw what they're working on at the institute, my spirits fell quite a bit. They measure, record, plot graphs, write up reports . . . and that's it. And they're as far from practical telepathy as I am from that great discovery I dreamed of as a child."

They rested another two hours, talking about people, science, and the biotosis. Then they dressed and went back down into the quarry. Erik holed up in his tent to analyze the water samples. Sergei handled the biotosis. An hour of concentrated work passed.

"Eri! Hey, Eri!" Sergei suddenly shouted, cupping his dirty hands.

"What do you want?" Erik's glasses flashed angrily from the dark entrance to the tent.

"Come here! Hurry!"

When Erik got there, Sergei pointed at the rosy mass in the net.

"Look!"

"What?"

"There are two pieces of the biotosis in here. I ran out of netting, so I put them in together. They're growing four times faster than the separate ones."

"How did you determine that?"

"By weighing, direct weighing following the methods of old man Lavoisier. It shows that the doubled biotosis grows four times faster."

Erik was lost in thought. His thinking process was swift and feverish.

He wriggled his fingers impatiently.

"That means. . . ."

"That means that we should pile the rest of the biotosis into the net and see what happens," Sergei said.

"Fine."

"But hurry it up, because it's getting dark and it looks like rain."

Erik looked up. There was a small malevolent cloud on the edge of the quarry. The dark-blue bottom of the cloud testified to its intentions. Erik pictured the cold streams of water pouring from the heavens, pouring down the steep slopes of the quarry, and he shuddered.

"Do we have time?"

"Yes, but hurry."

They ran to the nets stretched across the stream. Sergei pulled out the stakes, undid the simple knots, and handed the ends to Erik. He slowly transported the buoyant biotosis downstream. Twenty minutes later the pinkish pieces of the biotosis were untied and laid to rest in a regular geometrical pattern on three nets in the widest part of the stream.

"Grow," Sergei said, covering the flower with a cloth.

"Just made it," Erik added, shaking the first raindrops from his face.

They gave their baby one last look and ran up to the house.

It got dark. The dark clouds fell to earth and began whipping it with streams of water. As far as the eye could see, everything was covered with a murky foam of impotent frenzy. When Sergei opened the window, the rain brought the smell of the storm into the room.

"I hope the biotosis holds," Erik said and suddenly smacked his forehead. "What about the spectrograph? It'll get flooded."

"It'll be fine. The tent is waterproof."

The storm winked with lightning, thundered threats, and grumbled for some time before finally weakening and dying down.

It was quiet. They could hear the heavy drops falling from the roof and the rustle of the wind, lazily floating in the steppe night.

"I'll go down and see how things are," Erik said.

"Forget it, you'll see tomorrow. Look how dark it is."

Sergei went to bed. Erik sat by the window and stared out into its inky expanse for a long time.

Sergei woke up in the middle of the night with a jolt. He thought that someone was screaming. The voice was far away.

Sergei jumped up and started pulling his clothes on in the dark. Before he was dressed, something happened. The darkness disappeared and Sergei saw a bright-red control panel with many dials and quivering needles. There was a transparent plastic wall over the panel, and beyond it the earth was whirling and flying off somewhere, showing dark green through the pale cloud cover. Sergei realized that he was at the controls of a plane, and he confidently pulled the steering wheel toward himself. He knew just what he was doing. The plane leveled.

Suddenly Sergei felt that he was lying on hot sand. The sky above was a deep blue, bluer than he had ever seen. The blinding sun bore down on him like a Cyclops' eye. There was a smell of smoke and a babble of voices. Sergei sat up and looked at himself. He saw his body, naked, completely black, his tightly bound feet, his jutting ribs, the rags on his slim hips. . . . Late at night he was lying in a ditch on a narrow side street, and he was being kicked by iron-tipped shoes. His torturers spoke Italian, and he could understand them. . . .

Then unfamiliar, un-Russian faces, cars, grape vines, and a house with transparent walls and ceiling flashed by, and they all blended into a brilliant, spinning carousel. His last sensation was of being held by the feet. Sergei was hanging upside down, completely naked and wet, and he was screaming. He knew very well that he had been born a long time ago, and yet he couldn't rid himself of the feeling that it had just happened.

Then everything disappeared. Sergei was in the dark room of the biostation with his pants in his hands. The vision hadn't lasted more than a second.

His head was spinning and his ears were ringing. His muscles were contorted, as though by a weak convulsion.

"Eri! Eri!"

The moans faded in the black stillness of the room. There was no answer. Sergei called Erik once more. Silence. He slowly pulled on his clothes with stiff fingers and carefully took a step.

"Erik!"

A gust of cool air rushed in the open door. Sergei went outside. The night was still and dark; there was a sharp smell of dampness, and bright stars littered the puddles.

"Erik!"

Sergei took a few steps forward. For some reason he felt marvelous. His tension had eased and he felt relaxed. He breathed deeply. He was surprised by the lightness of his body, it felt weightless. He hurried to the quarry. And interestingly, he felt no anxiety. His own feelings engrossed him. He could not concentrate on what had happened to Erik. He was distracted by the amazing lightness of his body, and the sensation of unusual strength in his hands, legs, chest—his whole body.

Going down the path, he froze for a few seconds. Even in the thick southern night he could see that the pit had disappeared. In its place was a huge white mass that looked like frozen smoke. At first Sergei thought that it had snowed. In August? Then he decided that there had been an earthquake and the soil had been churned up. But the mountain looming over him did not resemble an unplanned pile of dirt. It looked more like a cloud that had fallen to earth. A weak cold light shone under its dull surface. There was a strange perfume in the air.

The biotosis?

Sergei rushed toward it, feeling the cool, slippery curves of the polymer.

"Erik! Erik!"

He ran around the circumference of the biotosis, splashing puddles and stars. In one spot, where the edge of the polymer did not quite reach the slope of the pit, forming a black crack, he heard a low moan. Sergei slipped in, pushed aside the soft mass, and squeezed inside. He felt Erik's head and shoulders. He was lying on a flat box. Sergei slowly pulled his friend from under the sticky weight of the polymer. He noted with wonder the ease with which he overcame its sticky resistance.

Erik did not stir. He must have been unconscious for a long

time. Sergei lifted his inert body and headed back to the station.
In the bright light Erik's sunken cheeks and closed eyes terrified Sergei. He fluffed the pillow and put Erik's hands on top
of the blanket.

Suddenly he felt a strange weakness. The room spun before his eyes, and he had to sit down to keep from falling. He
felt sick. After two minutes, he forced himself to get up and go
into the next room. He felt a little better in there.

The syringe and the medicines were in the refrigerator. Sergei
turned on the chemical sterilizer and came back into Erik's room
a few minutes later with everything necessary for the shot. Erik
lay deathly still.

Sergei exposed his friend's right arm, swabbed the inside of
his elbow with alcohol, and gave him the shot. And he immediately felt a sharp pain in his right arm. He put down the
syringe and rolled up his sleeve. There was a dark spot on his
pale skin and a small drop of blood had appeared in it. Sergei
examined it with fear and disbelief. He had given Erik the shot
—why did he also feel the pain?

The weakness hit him again. It felt as though he had fallen
into a deep hole. Clutching the walls, Sergei went outside.

Chapter 2

KARABICHEV WAS NOTHING like what Sergei imagined; Sergei, as usual, had been one-sided and prejudiced in his assessments. Karabichev's clear mind did not wander in the dark reaches of association, searching for the mysterious properties of things. He saw things the way they were. And no one in the world could possibly make him think about causes and effects that he could not experience himself.

His meeting with Sergei in front of the Mars Cinema had left an impression. But the only aspect that he had understood completely was Sergei's frank sympathy. Not that Sergei had uttered a single word of sympathy, but Karabichev understood everything that the other man had wanted to say. However, Sergei was wrong in thinking that Karabichev had "screamed." As usual, Sergei was judging people by his own standards. Sergei

43

had needed that scream of Karabichev's to support his own deeply
personal feelings about people.

In August, Karabichev was also on vacation, and he went
south to stay with his wife's relatives. The village of Pronok was
situated on the tiny Prona River, whose banks were overgrown
with willow. Karabichev would spend the whole day in the far
reaches of the river and come home at night with a pathetic
catch, tired but happy. Methodical, calm Karabichev, who had
his worms arranged by size and color and who imposed a process
he called "soupification" on his catch, could spend days at a spot
where the last known catch was recorded 150 years ago.

That morning Karabichev was planning to go to a grassy knoll
that he loved and had long ago put on his list of scenic fishing
sites. The river bank descended to the water in a sharp and unexpected drop. Although it was long past the time to get out
of bed, check his fishing gear, have a glass of cold milk with a
piece of black bread, and head out across the dewy grass, shiver-
ing in the chilly air, Karabichev couldn't wake up. His head was
off the pillow, and he was snoring, moaning, and suffocating, as
though a bulldozer were on his chest. Something similar was
happening to his wife. She was crying out in her sleep.

Karabichev opened his eyes and sat up, looking around in
amazement. He did not recognize the bedroom and seemed not
to remember where he was. He stared at his tanned wrists,
touched the blanket, and listened to Maria's mumbling.

"A nightmare," he whispered, shaking his head.

Then he got up and walked across the room, his feet absorbing the cool freshness of the floor. He stopped, thought, and
said aloud: "I am Andrei Anatolyevich Karabichev, I am Andrei
Anatolyevich Karabichev. . . ."

In the morning stillness his voice was unexpectedly loud.

I need . . . air, he decided.

A saving thought. He gathered his things with brusque movements and left without his milk and bread. The streets were
empty. The village was still asleep. The sun was rising far away,
and the pushy rays were getting into chinks in the fences and in
between the leaves.

Karabichev walked along the dusty sidewalk, telling himself

how good he felt, how pleasant it was, and how much better it would be.

There was a woman walking in front of him. She was balancing two pails of milk on a yoke across her shoulders. Young, heavy-set, and very serene, she rolled along the side street, a ball of quiet and warm happiness. When he came abreast of her, Karabichev glanced at her rosy cheeks and turned away.

Suddenly he saw himself. He had never seen himself so strangely, so alien to himself, in any mirror in his life. An olive-green jacket, tall zippered boots, backpack, a swaggering confident gait. He saw his head, large and handsome, on a long neck, turning to the side with a sharp energetic movement. Simultaneously, Karabichev felt that his body had gotten flabby and heavy, that a puff of soft hair had fallen on his back, that his shoulders were bent under the weight of the yoke. He remembered a completely unfamiliar kitchen, where a clumsy pale boy was sitting at a low table, spooning the remains of cereal from his bowl into his plump funnel-shaped mouth. The boy's name was Vladik, and the name created a pleasant pain in Karabichev's heart and made him want to smile. And at the same time he relived the full horror of his nightmare. He wanted to run, to get away from the frightening Karabichev who was coming at him with fishing poles that looked like Cossack spears. But his long skirt got in the way. Karabichev took another step.

The invasion stopped. The woman with the pails remained behind him.

When he got to the turnoff, Karabichev looked back. The woman was walking, swaying in rhythm with her burden. Karabichev turned down the street that led to the river. The woman walked a few more steps, then stopped, set her milk pails on the ground, and stared after the vanished Karabichev. She heaved a long sigh, wiped the sudden sweat from her face, and went on her way.

Karabichev fought his way through the thick growth of nettles by the river. There was a fine blue mist over the water. The trees on the banks cast their shapeless shadows on the river, which reeked of dampness and rotting algae. Karabichev didn't undo his line. He tossed the poles into the wet grass and sat down, leaning against his backpack. He silently watched the dark ripples.

The sun rose higher. Karabichev could feel its hot rays on his face, but he did not budge. He kept looking down to the place where the shadows of the grasses and trees grew shorter, until they disappeared from the water completely.

Full day came. Hot, lazy, and debilitating, it crawled out and lay down on the ground, starting up the crickets' hysterical chatter. The sun floated and melted in the sky. It grew hotter.

When it got intolerable, Karabichev stripped and swam a short distance in the cold water. As he dressed, he stopped for a second and spoke out loud:

"Have I gone crazy?"

And he quickly looked around.

Maybe someone was eavesdropping.

He got back toward evening, when the heat dozed and the steppe cooled off.

As he approached the village he felt the anxiety again. He did not want to go there. He could hear noise coming from the depths of the winding streets. Karabichev felt slightly dizzy, for he hadn't eaten all day.

The first person he met was a seven-year-old boy. The boy was pulling a rocket on wheels and crying bitterly. Karabichev patted his blond curls; he wanted to ask the child something when he suddenly felt an acute resentment against his mama, who had just whaled his behind. Karabichev felt the tears streaming down his face and his mouth contorting into a mortally offended pretzel. He jumped back from the boy in terror. The frightened boy, Goga (Karabichev realized that that was his name), ran away like the wind, dragging his beat-up rocket. Karabichev looked after him in despair. He was beginning to be afraid of people. Every time he saw someone, he shuddered and quickly crossed to the other side of the street. He took the most out-of-the-way side streets to get home. But even so, as he strode along the soft dusty earth he sensed that something bad was happening in the village. Shouts, laughter, and curses came from darkened yards. A woman howled somewhere. It was terrifying—a long human howl escaped from the darkness and ran into the purple sky.

Karabichev ran. He wanted to get home as soon as possible. "Maria . . . you'll understand me. I think I'm in big trouble." He ran right into a group of teenagers who had appeared in the darkness.

"You're ours! You're ours!" They chanted and danced in a circle around him. Karabichev was dumbfounded. A kaleidoscope of unbelievable sensations swirled in his body. Like that morning, he could see himself with his backpack, fishing poles, and boots, but this time he could see the back of his head and his face, his back and his chest, his arms and his legs, all of himself at once. A strange and amazing feeling: he was no longer Andrei Anatolyevich Karabichev. He had disappeared, dissolved in the laughing faces, in the supple dancing figures. He wanted to spin faster, even though he was standing still. He could feel pain in his wrists from his partners' strong hands, even though he was standing alone in the middle of the circle.

With a moan, Karabichev pushed his way through the group and found himself free. The crowd of laughing teenagers ran on.

So that's it, thought Karabichev. It only happens when people are nearby, up close. Step back a few feet, and it's like it never happened. I have to remember that.

He reached the house at dark. Thank God, there was no one in the yard or on the porch. Karabichev looked in the window. Maria was sitting at the table in the brightly lit room, cupping her chin in her hands. Her gaze moved dreamily along the simple pattern of the tablecloth. She looked into the mirror and wrinkled her face in disgust.

My wife, the person closest to me in the world. You've always understood me, and you'll understand now. I shouldn't have run away from you this morning. I could have used your help. I was a fool. But it's all right now. . . .

Maria got up and took several steps, swaying her hips. She abruptly reached for a cigarette and lit it.

Karabichev couldn't put his finger on what was wrong at first. Then he remembered. Maria had never smoked in her life! He rushed to the room and ran against the locked door. He slammed his shoulder into the door until it opened.

"Maria!"

His wife dropped her cigarette on the floor and stared at him in silence. Her face was terribly pale and tense, her lips parted.

Karabichev looked at her. His wife's face seemed unfamiliar and alien. It frightened him.

"Maria!"

A flicker of madness crossed Maria's eyes. She turned and said confusedly:

"*Je ne vous connais pas.*"

Karabichev was dumbstruck. Maria spoke a few other phrases in French. Karabichev couldn't even imagine what to think.

"Maria, Maria, calm down. Remember. I'm your husband, Andrei," he muttered.

Maria stared at him intently. A light glimmered in her eyes. She even whispered something familiar and tender. And then she began talking even louder and less coherently. Blotches covered her face, her chest heaved. Karabichev had never seen her this way. An unfamiliar angry fold settled in between Maria's eyebrows and her rounded mouth scattered words like resonant buckshot.

The table lamp glowed under its perylon shade. Maria's family squeezed into a frame on the wall. A fly, stuck between the window frames buzzed angrily. A dog with the immortally clever name of Spot yelped under the window.

Karabichev took a step forward and embraced his wife. Maria froze. They stood locked in each other's arms for a few seconds. Silence enveloped them like an eiderdown. Someone was crying in the hall, and Karabichev could hear muffled sobs.

And then a current ran through their bodies. They jumped back away from each other, angrily staring straight ahead. Karabichev now knew. The woman remained. She sank to a chair and wrung her hands.

Karabichev went out on the porch. In the dark, he could make out a shapeless dark form huddled on the stoop. It was his mother-in-law, Evgeniya. She was weeping, and Karabichev could hear her tearful words:

"Maria, my darling little daughter."

Karabichev said in a trembling voice, "You no longer have a daughter, Evgeniya. And I don't have my wife Maria. We now have Mademoiselle Dittie LeBrun, a French girl of twenty-three."

He walked around his mother-in-law carefully and went down the pale path.

The stars in the black sky seemed too big and unnaturally bright. The luminescent street lamps swayed, casting an uneven light on the sidewalk. The street looked like the deck of a ship during a storm. A light evening breeze carried danger and icy despair.

Karabichev walked several blocks and stopped in front of a small house hidden under a canopy of dusty acacias. Instead of a nameplate there was a simple electric buzzer on the old doors. Karabichev pressed it. Auntie Glasha appeared in the doorway, a distant relative of the doctor, Petr Mikhailovich Gorin. She spread her hands in answer to his question:

"Of course not, dearie, no. He's at the clinic. Such goings-on here! The hospital is overcrowded, the doctors can barely stand on their feet. Has something terrible happened to you, too?"

Karabichev shrugged.

"There is something. I'd like to talk it over with Petr."

"Well, then, come on in." Auntie Glasha bustled around. "You haven't been to see us in a long time. Just can't keep away from your fishing. Come on, I'll give you some tea."

The old woman obviously needed someone to talk to. Karabichev, keeping his distance, followed.

"How's Maria?" Auntie Glasha asked.

Karabichev lowered his head.

"I see. There are strange things happening to many folk now. It began this morning. Even before that, at dawn. Take our neighbor, for instance. Has a wife, three children. He's a good man, hard worker. Doesn't drink. And today he made such a scene, you should have heard him. He started shouting that they're not his children and that's that! He chased his wife out, saying he didn't want to know her. She's a stranger, she was unfaithful. They've lived together for twenty years, and he says he doesn't know her! But as for the playing around, well, he opened our eyes with that. You'd never have suspected. She's a quiet, modest woman. . . . Of course it's easier for religious people to bear any kind of upheaval. They have a foundation."

"When do you expect Petr?"

"I don't know, sir. They're bringing him sick people in droves today. Such goings-on."

Karabichev had a glass of strong tea, leafed through a medical journal, and stopped to think. Unhappy thoughts were racing through his mind. A loud voice rang out in the hallway: Petr Mikhailovich, a sturdy sexagenarian with ruddy cheeks and a shiny pate in a nimbus of white hair, came into the room with his assistant, Anastasia Sveshnikova.

"Andrei! Glad to see you. I won't shake hands for obvious reasons. Politeness right now is impoliteness. Sit down, my friends. It's been a hard day, and it's not over. I think that the night will bring us new surprises. Don't you think so, Anastasia?"

The young woman nodded seriously, and her glasses gleamed in the light. Karabichev asked:

"Can you explain what's happening, Petr?"

"First tell me what your problem is," the doctor replied.

Karabichev told him. When he told him about himself, the doctor nodded as though he had known all along. But when Karabichev began telling him about his wife, the doctor's attention heightened. He exchanged looks with his assistant and they listened attentively to the end of Karabichev's story.

"We haven't seen anything like that today," Petr said, getting up. "But that's not important now. Something else is important now. . . ."

He crossed the study to the window and raised the blind.

"There, my friends, you have probably the quietest village in our region. Dear old Pronok, you dozed on the banks of the charming Prona River. You have been only slightly affected by civilization, technology, automation, and progress. You buy television sets and aerocars, but you're not interested in obtaining heavy water. You gobbled up megavitamins, but you couldn't care less about rocketry. You preferred animal husbandry to cybernetics, and grapes to atomic energy. Even nuclear tests didn't disturb your well-deserved sleep. Even the landing of the space ship from Venus didn't turn you from your stubborn agricultural ways. And now, look. This oasis of peace and quiet is turbulent, buzzing like a disturbed beehive. It's one o'clock in the morning, but lights are on everywhere. Do you hear those voices, those screams, the laughter, the crying, and all the strange noises? Do you hear all that? What does it all mean? Pronok has awakened! It has gotten a good swift kick!"

Petr sat down.

"I don't know what's going on," he said, sighing, "but it's clear to me that some spring has broken in the universe or else a new one has appeared. All the people in the world, do you understand, everybody—in Pronok, in Moscow, in London, in Washington...."

"Do you really mean that this is everywhere?" Karabichev asked.

"That's the point, my dear friend. It's everywhere. Haven't you been listening to the radio? The governments of the socialist countries have already made appeals to their people."

"I wasn't here. I ran away into the country. I thought that I was the only madman."

"This as yet nameless psychosis has affected all of humanity. Of course, it manifests itself differently in different places. You should have seen the hundreds of patients I had today. But the most frightening part is that they're not sick. They are absolutely healthy. They have no business in either a hospital or a clinic. I told our party organizer that I would refuse to see them. Why should all those beaten wives, rejected husbands, parents who don't recognize their children, and casual lovers be brought to me? He says that I'm obliged to see everyone who comes to me. But I moved closer to him, and I could tell he was lying to me and that he felt exactly the same way that I did. He realized that I had found him out, and he laughed and said: 'What else are we to do, Petr, what else?' And then I sensed what a pleasant man this was. I felt as warm as if I had had a shot of cognac. And before the only words I had for him were 'bureaucrat' and 'form-filler.' That's some disease for you. Even if it is a sickness it's not fatal. I told an operator from the meat-packing plant that he had nothing to complain of—a heart like a bull, reflexes perfectly normal, and a nervous system that would be the envy of any pilot, so there was nothing to worry about. And he told me that he was 'all screwed up.' 'My wife knows everything about me, and I know everything about her, and I can't understand where I stop and she begins. Sometimes I feel like messing around in the kitchen, or trying on hats, or some nonsense just gets into my head.' "

"I experienced something quite similar," Karabichev confessed sheepishly.

"Yes." Gorin smiled. "The most unexpected things happen." He looked long and hard at his assistant.

"But, what is the nature of all this ... sickness?" Karabichev asked.

The old man shrugged.

"Unknown. The Americans are shouting that it's an epidemic spread by Soviet biologists. Some virus that bites everyone at once. Nonsense, of course. No microbe can circle the earth in a few hours. And anyway, what kind of sickness is it, if people remain perfectly healthy? There are no physical or psychological malfunctions observed."

"People just feel 'screwed up,' " Anastasia added softly.

"Yes, 'screwed up,' but nobody knows just how as yet. People seem to be asleep when they're wide-awake. They remain themselves but at the same time they become other people—the people next to them. All this happens without words, without any effort on the part of people. If a person is in a crowd the world starts to double, triple, quadruple. There seems to be a layering of psychic worlds."

"Or a strong displacement."

"Yes. Or that. But beyond a distance of four to six feet the effect of mutual overlay disappears. A person becomes himself again. And that's all. I prescribe that my patients stay far away from each other, and everything will be all right."

"Let's listen to the radio?" Anastasia suggested.

She turned on the set. Agitated foreign speech burst into the room.

"What should I do with Maria?" Karabichev asked quietly.

Gorin looked at him seriously.

"There is no medicine and there's no prescription. There is only logic. Let her listen to radio transmissions from Paris, then she'll get some idea of the situation. Talk to her in French. If you don't know the language well enough, ask someone to help.

Try to elicit some memories related to her habits, her feelings—
her clothing, familiar shoes. Try kissing her."

"I can't, she's a stranger," Karabichev said.

Petr Mikhailovich raised his eyebrows.

"Pardon, we're talking about your wife."

"Nothing of the kind. She's Dittie LeBrun. Where's Maria?
Her body has stayed behind, and even that's not her body anymore."

The radio announcer was speaking German. Karabichev knew
German, and he listened.

"This is Vienna. We are reporting on the events of the second half of August 15, 19—."

"Last night?" Karabichev whispered.

"Yes," Gorin replied. "The horror happened last night."

The radio announcer continued. People had found themselves
outside of space and time. All the usual references and norms
had been destroyed and overturned. A pilot, flying a jet at high
altitude, had felt that he was lying in a bathtub and started to
feel around for his soapy sponge, letting go of the controls.
There had been more aerocar and automobile accidents in ten
hours than in the last five years. People had let go of steering
wheels, pressed the wrong buttons, fooled with the pedals, braked
at full speed. People had fallen out of open windows, walked
across railings and barriers, hurting themselves seriously or mi-
raculously sustaining only light injuries.

The world of generally accepted concepts had been destroyed
in each person. Shards of logic and causality swirled like black
ashes in the confused brain of humanity.

It was a universal mirage that attacked children and adults,
men and women, military and civilian personnel, idiots and
scholars. Every person, in a few seconds of an unrepeatable dream,
had experienced a long shattering journey through the souls of
other people.

A bureaucrat who had never taken his eyes from the top of
his polished desk had seen volcanic lava, foaming, strong-smelling,
inexorably creeping up to his feet. A young woman had become
an old man; a child, an adult. Men had become infants, blacks
had become white, whites had become black, and atheists had

become priests. A tornado of fragmented, fleeting, and often vague images had passed through people's organisms. Austrian scientists were stressing the word "organisms" because everyone who had lived through the night of August 15 maintained that they not only had seen the illusions that had appeared before them but had also smelled, touched, and heard them. The sense of reality was so strong that many of those who had made the nocturnal trip had returned with "physical proof." Bruno B. showed two black eyes allegedly received in a street brawl somewhere on the Cape of Good Hope. Josif S., a chemical engineer, had not slept the night of August 15; he was playing poker. Just before dawn, he had suddenly seen himself on an operating table. They were doing a stomach resection. The operation was torture. When he awoke he was with his friends, cards in hand. The vision had lasted no more than ten seconds. A sharp pain made Josif lie down. Feeling his stomach, he found a scar that had not been there before.

There were close to a thousand similar examples. Information was coming in about similar cases in Europe, America, Asia, Africa, and Australia. Some of the facts were funny, and others were sad. But all the information had one thing in common that was leading scientists to hope that they would be able to find the cause of the "great madness." That common factor was the brevity of the nightmare's action. In individual cases, it had been so brief that it hadn't even been noticed. In others, it had lasted a minute and a half to two minutes. The brevity and simultaneity of the visions permitted scientists, doctors, and biologists to concentrate their efforts on a limited front of research.

The problem was that the nightmare was not over. It remained in the form of a special effect, the mutual-overlay effect, or, the W-effect. There were definite moral difficulties related to the effect, but they were not yet clear. Stanislaus Samovyak, a doctor, categorically rejected the possibility of an epidemic nature of the W-effect, proposed by the American Paul Johnson. No virus could—

"What did I tell you!" Gorin exclaimed joyfully. "An obvious point. No one doubted for a minute that it's not viruses."

Karabichev got up determinedly, as though he had found a solution and was ready to act.

"I'll be going, Petr," he said, taking a step toward the old man and extending his hand. He realized what he was doing, but it was too late. He saw pure love. His heart contracted deliciously, a light sadness crept up toward his throat, and languor oozed throughout his body. Karabichev stood there, moved and embarrassed. It was like being in an April shower. He looked at Anastasia and only then realized that she was sitting very close to Gorin, much closer than the prescribed six feet.

"That's how it is," Petr Mikhailovich said in a trembling voice. "Some find sorrow, and we ... it's completely different for us. We've worked together for five years and literally never saw each other. And today ... we saw."

"That's good, that's very good," Karabichev muttered and left.

He walked down the dark street with a springy step, pushing the earth down away from his feet into the bottomless universe. As he walked his movements became clearer and clearer. Action, he had to act! Before, when he thought that he was alone, he had the right to worry about himself, but now, when there were millions, he had to do everything to help them and himself.

There was a small crowd at the phone center. Karabichev was immediately struck by its uniqueness. No one was standing near anyone else. They all kept six feet between them.

Polite, aren't they, Karabichev thought, smiling to himself.

It wasn't easy to reach Moscow. Karabichev spent a long time in the glass booth watching the blinking blank screen. The voice in the phone kept saying: "Please wait, the line is busy. . . . Please wait. . . . Please wait."

Finally, there was a click, and the screen lit up with a blue light.

"I'm connecting you," the girl forty kingdoms away said.

Ermolov's deformed face appeared on the screen. He didn't listen to Karabichev. His resonant bass filled the booth.

"I'm glad you called. We really need you here. Leave immediately. How are things with you?"

Karabichev answered with a wave of the hand.

"Maria's bad."

"Bring her with you. Things are almost back to normal in Moscow. It was a real nightmare last night and this morning, but now it's all right. We've organized a commission to study this phenomenon at the institute. Its magnitude is unbelievable, but I guess you've already heard. Read the announcement—there are many important things in it. So long."

He disappeared. Karabichev set off for home with a heavy heart. It was difficult there. No one had gone to bed; everyone was afraid of a repetition of last night's nightmare. Dittie Le-Brun, or Maria Karabicheva, was sitting on the sofa. Karabichev noted with surprise that she looked even less like his wife. It was the same Maria, but her cheeks were sunken, there were shadows under her eyes, her full lips had been compressed into a thin line, and her movements had become abrupt and sharp.

Karabichev, overcoming his desire to get as far away from all of this as possible, took down the Russian-French dictionary and began talking with Mademoiselle LeBrun. Their dialogue was punctuated with exclamations of disbelief, shrugged shoulders, and sarcastic looks. Just when he thought he had managed to explain something about psychic transmutation to her, she would shake her head and say that she understood nothing. Then he dragged her into Evgeniya's room, where there was a big old radio. They managed to tune in Paris, and Maria was transformed. Hearing French, Maria wept. She was gradually becoming sadder. The amazing event that humanity had lived through was beginning to get through to her consciousness.

Karabichev tried to comfort Evgeniya, who was crying bitterly, and watched Maria, who was rapturously listening to distant Paris, and thought how all this was crazy, absurd, and impossible.

He went out on the porch and listened to the still sounds of the night. The deep velvety black of the sky and the sleeping damp earth stretched out before him. But Karabichev took no notice of his surroundings. He was troubled by other images.

Everything was mixed up. The possible and the impossible. Skyscrapers toppled. Streets buckled toward the sky. Window glass no longer let through light. Ocean liners tiptoed on land on spindly legs. You could grab a star from the red skies, but there was no way of knowing whether you could light a regular match.

Someone touched Karabichev's shoulder. Dittie LeBrun, tears in her eyes, stood before him. Trying to speak French slowly and distinctly, she apologized. Now she understood many things. She had some medical knowledge. Such sorrow.

Karabichev sighed and asked Mademoiselle LeBrun to accompany him to Moscow in the morning. She nodded.

Chapter 3

Ruzhena liked her equipment. She saw it as being very gentle, kind, and obedient. The winking lights and quivering dials, the smell of heated insulation told the young woman more than words could about the inner state of the wise machines. When she came into her lab in the morning, she would first clean up, then check the health of her apparatus, and only then begin the day's scheduled research.

Ruzhena liked her work. She liked spending hours creating miniature sets, soldering connections, wrapping the almost invisible springs of the weights; the constructions of tiny parts looked like abstract sculptures. Sometimes Ruzhena wore large glasses during her experiments, and then the outside world ceased to exist for her. She would lose herself in her work. Everyone knew

58

that glasses on Ruzhena's nose meant that she was completely cut off from reality.

In the tense days after August 15, Ruzhena continued her regular study of several telepathic parameters. She showed up by nine, donned her snow-white lab coat, and spent a few minutes studying the field of the upcoming battle. After Sergei left on vacation, the glasses appeared more frequently on her nose. Adjusting the heavy frames, she sighed softly.

A sharp rap made her jump. Ermolov's face appeared on the screen.

"Ruzhena, there's a meeting of the committee members today. Attendance is mandatory."

"But—"

"No buts—unless you want a chewing out. Please be there by ten."

The screen went out, as though someone had splashed ink on it. Ruzhena shrugged and took off the lab coat. Today would be wasted. She went downstairs. Several young telepathists were trying out new forms of communication on themselves: the young men and women sat in a circle on low stools and moved closer to and farther away from each other. There was much laughter and shouting.

"That's terrific! I had no idea it was possible!"

"But the reception is still bad. There's still some vagueness."

"That's because she's a woman. And even a supertelepathic device will never figure out a woman."

Once in a while there would be a reminder like:

"Hey, Watch the dirty stuff in public. Porno is strictly forbidden!"

Ruzhena watched them with a smile, hesitant about joining their bubbling enthusiasm.

A tall, stoop-shouldered man walked into the room and asked in a squeaky voice, "What's this bedlam?"

They called out as soon as they saw him.

"Come on, you pathetic theoretician! We'll show you that there are no antipathetic souls in the world. Come on. Everybody's sympathetic. Put him in the middle, let him dissolve for a while, that'll get him off his high horse."

They grabbed him and pulled him into the circle.

"Halt, children of Aeolus, halt!" he shouted. "Doesn't the condemned get to say anything?"

"Go ahead." The masses had spoken.

"Before you subject me to the most horrible punishment that a human intellect has ever received," he said, sitting down at a distance from the telepathists (Ruzhena remembered his name— it was Shchapov), "and force me to dissolve in the morass of your conceited and prideful souls, I must relate the following story, which befell the wonderful Shchapov this morning. It—"

"—is a shaggy-dog story. You get only three minutes. Or else we'll centrifugate you."

"Centrifugation" consisted of placing a person in the center of a circle of dancers who spun around him until he lost his orientation and his ability to comprehend anything.

"Wait a minute!" Shchapov shrieked. "Hear me out. And you will be blessed. So, today the wonderful Shchapov, arising from his bed, in which he saw nothing either sinful or forbidden, headed for. . . ."

The story boiled down to the fact that on the way to the institute, Shchapov had met a man who was barely able to stand up.

"I don't know why the guy had been boozing, but he was blotto. And I, at the urgings of some inner voice, followed him. At first, I kept the safe distance, but then . . . I violated it. I got right behind him. And he and I walked a few bus stops. By the end of that little trek I was just as drunk as my pal. The earth swayed under my feet and my ears buzzed. I showed up at the institute singing 'Sweet Adeline.' My friends, I have made a major discovery! We can bring the production of alcoholic spirits down to a minimum. You need only one really good drunk per city for all the inhabitants to get soused. Unlicensed sale of alcohol! No expense on hors d'oeuvres! Telepathic inebriation! The cheapest in the history of mankind! How to satisfy five thousand thirsty people with one glass? Now this great problem has been solved. All you have to do is shake hands."

"Enough, enough! Let's shake up Shchapov! Don't forget to punish the inventor of free liquor. To keep others from trying it, too."

"Watch it, folks, watch it, I still have some of the inebriating

germs in me. Be careful, or you'll be singing 'Sweet Adeline'
yourselves."

Ruzhena looked at her watch and slipped out of the room. It
was three minutes of ten. Entering the half-empty auditorium,
she found herself a cozy spot behind a blue column and snuggled
in an armchair that was as soft and warm as a freshly baked pie.
The room slowly filled with the institute personnel. Ruzhena
could hear snatches of conversation:

"It's hard on our women. They're used to carrying around
loads of secrets, and now they're all out in the open. All the
seals are broken."

"Arkady Semyonovich went overboard. I just can't see it somehow...."

"Anything could happen nowadays. You should expect the
worst."

"How can it be any worse?"

"They say, in South America...."

It's all the same and yet somehow very different, thought
Ruzhena. People are on guard. They're afraid. Their words and
movements are uncertain.

Ermolov and his colleagues sat in the presidium. He straight
ened his square shoulders and plugged his yellow eyes into the
audience.

"Our institute committee is one of the sections of the United
Council on Studying the W-Effect, or as we call it, the mutual-
overlay effect. We have done much work in the last few days
in gathering and processing data on the dispersal of the effect. A
report on this matter will be given by...."

He named a worker at the institute. The man coughed and
began:

"The data reveal that this effect has spread universally. We
have received reports from the farthest corners of the globe. The
same thing is happening everywhere. However, the strength of
the mutual overlay varies. In South America and Australia the
effect is experienced even at a distance of ninety to a hundred
and fifty feet. In fact, people there are in a constant state of
unwilled communication. However, in Moscow and the middle
band of European Russia the overlay is observed only when

people get within thirty to thirty-six inches of each other. These data have made it possible to draw up a geographic map of the distribution of the mutual overlay effect."

He approached the world map, which was covered with concentric patterns that looked like ebbing waves. The central and smallest circle was situated in the southern part of the Pacific Ocean. The professor pointed at it.

"The strength is highest here. Every circle covers territory with the same strength. The farther from the center, the weaker the effect. As you see, Moscow is transected by the isotone for the weakest index of strength, which simplifies our life considerably."

He went on for a long time, listing the geographic place names where the original forms of mutual overlay occurred and citing the reports of foreign scientists, but Ruzhena was too excited to listen to him. She could not take her eyes off the little black circle on the blue expanse of the Pacific.

A half-formed speculation was troubling her. She squirmed impatiently in her chair and jumped up to address the presidium the second the speaker had uttered his concluding phrase.

"Don't you think that the source of the emanations is in this spot in the Pacific Ocean?"

And then she noticed that everyone else in the auditorium was also on his feet and asking the same question. And Ermolov, the colleagues seated with him on the presidium, and the speaker himself were also repeating Ruzhena's question, maintaining its impatient interrogating tone.

Silence fell upon the room. The thought that came to everyone at once was formulated perfectly clearly.

Then the speaker laughed. Obviously things looked funnier from the podium than they did to the audience below. The auditorium erupted in loud guffaws as people laughed at the absurdity of their outburst.

They were embarrassed, and they teased each other with relief: "Arkady Semyonovich, such friskiness at your age? Eh? Where do you get your energy?"

Ermolov raised his hand.

"Dear comrades," he began in his deep voice, "apparently we were just victims of the W-effect ourselves. As you can see, its properties have not been adequately defined in a strict scientific sense. What just happened here could be termed a collective mutual overlay that occurred in a creative setting. There is nothing bad in this in the long run. Collective creativity among scholars is our dream. And it is coming true at a new level, of course, in a rather chaotic way that is not particularly pleasant for us. We do not know the cause of this phenomenon, and naturally, we are anxious. Such mystery makes the phenomenon undependable. We cannot be sure that the W-effect won't pull something else tricky on us. That is why the cause of this phenomenon worries all humanity. A week has passed since August 15. We are hearing about the most paradoxical manifestations of mutual overlay. Total or partial amnesia, transformation of personality, and so on. Scholars in every field and the people of every country in the world are trying to discover the source of the effect. The hypothesis of a disease caused by a new virus must be rejected. But we have just heard an interesting deduction. It sheds light on many of the mysterious aspects of the W-effect. By the way, I would like to suggest a simpler contraction. Instead of calling it the effect of mutual overlay, let's call it the EMO.

"Now, is it clear from Ivan Pavlovich's speech that EMO's influence on the population of the earth is regulated by an interesting law, and that there is a point of greatest intensity, located not far from Cape Horn.

"Comrades, this is a very important fact. I call the attention of everyone present to it. Even if we have not yet discovered the cause of EMO and have not found its source, at least to some degree of certainty we have determined its probable location. Right here." Ermolov traced the black circle on the map with his finger.

"I think that this will serve to answer the question that was stated by everyone present here today. We must send an expedition to that area of the globe, and we will do that. The United Council will aid us, and we will find the source of EMO!"

"I know what we'll find there!" The shout came from the audience. A tanned young man was pushing his way up the narrow aisle. He began speaking before he reached the podium.

"Forgive me for interrupting. I'm just very upset by Ivan Pavlovich's report. I'm sorry, I did interrupt, didn't I? Forgive me. So, comrades, this morning I heard on the radio that the American scientist Carlos Carlos attributes the existence of EMO, as we have named it, to the presence of aliens from outer space. He believes that they are already here and that this is the result of their action on us! They are communicating with us, and we don't understand them. And where are they? Well, right in that little circle in the Pacific Ocean!"

Pandemonium broke out. Everyone was shouting and jumping from his seat. Ruzhena leaped up too, surprised at herself. She shouted, waved her arms, and stamped her feet. Someone next to her was wailing with his hands folded in supplication: "It's not true, not true! The Czechs say it's a question of radiation. It's radiation, I tell you! Radiation!"

Ermolov disappeared. The only person left at the podium was the tanned young man who was waving his arms in agitation. The shouting increased. No one was listening to anyone else, and everyone was trying to drown out his neighbor. Ruzhena saw the wild eyes of professors, graduate students, and lab assistants—venerable old men and fuzzy-cheeked youths. She was also waving her arms and shouting, and she thought with fear, What is this? What's happening?

The general excitement reached an unbelievable pitch. The screams had blended into a single protracted wail. The doors of the auditorium opened, and the frightened faces that appeared in them were immediately sucked into the frenzied crowd, becoming as violent as the rest.

Ruzhena was gradually losing the ability to distinguish the faces of the people around her. They were shaking and jumping so hard that they blended into a vacillating, trembling membrane. It became intensely light, as though the sun had rolled into the room. The walls, the ceiling, the chairs, the people— all disappeared. The bright light blinded her. Ruzhena sensed a wild, uncontrollable surge of anger. She had to tear something. Her fingers, bent convulsively, were drawn to the sparkling curtain before her eyes. They met the desperate fingers of other people. Ruzhena pulled back her hands in surprise.

Karabichev had just arrived in Moscow with his wife, Maria/ Dittie LeBrun, and so he came to the institute later than usual.

He was told that all the senior scientists were at a committee meeting. Karabichev went up to the third floor, where the conference room was located, and saw that he was too late. The last of the audience was trickling out of the room. Ermolov walked right past him without stopping, merely waving hello. Ivan Pavlovich minced by with his tiny little steps. Karabichev stopped Ruzhena, who tried to sneak by unnoticed.

"Ruzhena, hello!"

The young woman stopped, embarrassed somehow. Karabichev noticed the red spots near her eyes and her dilated pupils.

"Ah, you're here already. That's good."

"Maybe. What was going here?"

"A meeting."

"About what?"

"Well. . . ." She thought for a bit. "We drafted a letter to the United Council. Actually, we thought about the best way to draft it. . . ."

"What's the letter about?"

"The letter? It's about . . . what's it called, the W-effect. Ermolov should know, he wrote the thing. You'd better ask him."

"All right, go on," Karabichev said angrily.

He peered into the conference room, hoping to find someone still there. It was empty. Karabichev was shocked by the condition of the room. The unsettled dust was swirling in the air in thick gray clouds, the chairs were piled up in several mounds, and some of them were broken. Karabichev walked across the dirty parquet floor, littered with papers and cigarette butts. This wasn't a meeting, it was a battle, he thought, coming up to the chairman's place. Strange, very strange.

He saw pieces of paper on the floor, torn and thoroughly trampled by many feet. He bent over and picked one up. Smoothing it with his fingers, he saw that it was a piece of a map. There was a thick black line drawn on it. Karabichev began picking up all the pieces.

When he entered Ermolov's office, Ermolov was standing by the window rubbing his temples.

"I'm glad that you've gotten here so fast. Sit down and talk."

Karabichev sat down and lit a cigarette. Ermolov paced impatiently.

"I must remember something," he said irritably. "And I just can't. It's right on the tip of my tongue, but I can't remember what it is! Damn it! All right, you say that your wife underwent a transformation? That's an unpleasant situation. But, unfortunately, it's not the only case. Who is she now? A Frenchwoman? Yes, that makes it difficult. But don't despair, all's not lost—"

Karabichev interrupted. "What letter were you drafting at the meeting today? Ruzhena told me about it, but I couldn't understand what it was all about."

"Letter? What letter? Oh, that's right. We were talking about some letter, but. . . ."

Ermolov was lost in thought.

"Hmm. I've forgotten. I think Ivan Pavlovich was writing it. Something unimportant. Actually, the meeting was a terrible waste of time. We needn't have had it."

"I hear it got rather noisy?"

"Noisy? Why, no . . . oh, I suppose so. Ivan Pavlovich really made us laugh. I can't remember just what it was . . . but the whole place was on the floor laughing."

Ermolov squirmed in his chair and said thoughtfully:

"I can't remember it. . . . And there's something spinning in my brain. Something important."

"Will this help you remember?" Karabichev asked calmly, getting up from his seat. He came up to the desk, moved the phone to one side, and emptied the pieces of paper on the glass top. Ermolov looked at him in amazement.

Karabichev silently matched up the pieces and smoothed them out until the world map appeared on the desk. Only the North Pole and a piece of Europe were missing.

"What is this?" Karabichev asked, pointing at the thick black circles that passed through the parallels and meridians. Ermolov said nothing. Karabichev looked at him. He was pale and tense. Suddenly he leaped at Karabichev.

"I remember, I remember!" Karabichev had never seen him look so disoriented. Ermolov's head and shoulders were shaking. "Oh, if you only could know what a horror it was! We tore up the map. We were mad. Ivan Pavlovich himself was tearing and trampling it. . . . Now I remember everything."

Ermolov described the mad scene in the conference room.

"Do you understand, it was like a wave that was carrying us. We couldn't resist."

"Mass hysteria?"

"Something like that, Andrei. First it was collective creativity, and then this mad ecstasy. We tore up the map for some reason.... I'm writing to the United Council right away to give them a detailed description of what happened at that meeting."

There was a long pause. Their thoughts were so horrible that neither could bring himself to utter them aloud.

"Listen, Andrei, I must ask you. Please don't say a word about this yet. People have forgotten, and that's fine. Let's not create a panic, all right?"

Karabichev looked into Ermolov's yellow eyes.

"But you will write to the United Council today, won't you?" he asked.

Ermolov reddened and turned away.

"Yes, of course," he said curtly.

Karabichev left Ermolov's office with a feeling of insecurity. Walking down the hall, he saw Ruzhena, peeking into a keyhole.

"Ruzhena!"

The young woman turned back quickly from the door.

"What are you doing?"

"Oh, I thought that someone was in there."

Karabichev tried the doorknob. The door was locked.

It was Sergei Arefyev's office. He had locked it when he left. Karabichev listened. There was silence on the other side of the door.

"Nonsense! I can't hear a thing. And if you're so interested in the room, get the key and open it. By the way, what have you heard from Sergei?"

They walked down the hall together.

"I've received several letters. He wrote that he and Erik were making great strides. Now their method can be applied industrially."

"And when do they plan to return?"

"They still have a lot of work—and Erik is very sick."

Karabichev looked at her.

"Then why doesn't he bring him here? They can help him here!"

Ruzhena shrugged.

"He writes that they have too many things to do."

"Can you phone there? Do they have a radiophone?"

"I don't know. He never told me."

"All right, I'll look into it."

Leaving Ruzhena, Karabichev opened his notebook and put "Sergei" with a question mark in his Important column. A crooked line connected several other notes, which included "Maria" and "Ermolov."

When he got home, Karabichev saw a letter on the shelf in the hall. It must have come yesterday. Karabichev picked up the letter and saw that it had a foreign postmark. "The West never leaves us" came to mind for some reason. The address was written in Russian in a familiar hand. He tore open the letter with trembling hands.

"My dearest Andrei!"

Dittie LeBrun heard a strange sound, dropped her face cream, and ran into the hall. Karabichev was rocking and moaning in a chair, as though in pain. The letter from Maria was clutched in his fist.

Chapter 4

THE FIELD was as flat as a drafting board. The small hillocks did not destroy the sense of endless plain. The huge mound that lay in the middle of the green frying pan made a strange, unexpected impression. It had no definite color and had absorbed all the rays and colors that were around it. On a hot day when the sky was clear and there was a lot of sun, it resembled a glistening iceberg with deep-blue shadows. In bad weather, the mound became gray and watery, looking like a storm cloud with a steely sheen. In the morning it was orange-yellow, and in the evening it glowed like a campfire in the setting sun's light.

"It has the shape of a flower," Erik said, looking at the sparkling mountain through the window. The biostation was now at its foot.

He was lying in a special scaffolding built by Sergei. Heavy splints supported his chest and shoulders.

"Did you hear me, Sergei? It looks like a flower!"

"Yeah, yeah," Sergei said, entering the room. "A flower that weighs a hundred million tons. I'd like to see the chest that could use it for a boutonnière. Or the nose that can take the perfume."

"We'll find them. What else is the chemical industry for?"

"Sorry to upset you, old buddy, but the tests show low durability. It's no polymer, it's more like jelly."

Erik was silent for a long time. Then he spoke, quietly, almost to himself:

"You know, sometimes I think that that's not the same biotosis that we came here with. I'm not even sure it's a biotosis at all."

Sergei raised his eyebrows angrily.

"The composition is the same, the structure is the same, the mineral additives are the same. What the hell kind of problems are you inventing now?"

"You see, I have a strange memory of that night. Of course, there's a lot that I didn't understand, because it all happened in a fraction of a second, but anyway—"

"Yeah, you've told me," Sergei said tiredly, sitting next to Erik. He rubbed his forehead, chasing away unpleasant thoughts.

"I had the feeling that all this hadn't risen up from the pit but had fallen from the sky. It may have seemed that way to me because of the rain and the speed of the biotosis' growth, but the feeling was definitely like this: clouds of hard smoke fell from above and buried me."

"A subjective impression." Sergei dismissed it. "Only one thing worries me. How could it have grown like that? It's making us look stupid. We grow over a hundred million tons of polymer and we don't know how. In fact, we're still right where we started, even though in theory we have succeeded."

"Why do you keep harping on a hundred million tons? Where did you get that figure?"

"Very simple. I calculated the volumes of the quarry and the mound now formed by the biotosis. We know the specific gravity—it's close to one. Multiply it and you'll get a hundred

and something million tons. Of course, that's rounded off. But
the point isn't in absolute figures anyway, but in the order of
magnitude. What miracle changed a few pounds into a million
tons?"

"That part is easy to explain. The basic raw material for the
biotosis' growth is the atmosphere, its gases. The possibilities
are unlimited. And the speed of the reaction depends on the
stage of development of the process. In this case the chain and
highly branched process led to the rapid development of the
biotosis."

"Then why did its growth cease so abruptly?" Sergei asked.
"According to my observations, it's stopped growing."

Erik thought.

"Maybe it's a question of energy?" he said, wiggling his stif-
fened fingers. "There was a heat loss into the surrounding
medium. How about that?"

"Maybe," Sergei said. "It just may be."

"You know, Sergei, we have the wrong approach to our biotosis.
We keep thinking about our strictly utilitarian goal—to obtain
a sturdy polymer and turn it over to industry. And we keep
looking at the real miracle that has occurred before our very eyes
in the same old way—how to get some use out of it as fast as
possible. I think the phenomenon of the biotosis' sudden growth
is considerably more complex, and as scientists, we should analyze
it thoroughly."

"That's all true. If the biotosis had grown like this six months
ago, I would be digging around in it myself with pleasure until
I found out what had happened, where the dead blob got the
energy. But the times have changed. Amazing things are happening in the world. To tell the truth, I'd like to be taking part
in them. And I'm irritated by this mountain of watery gelatin,
which has turned out to be completely different from what we
had thought. And then, you're hurt, and seriously, and we need
to get you out of here."

"I'm not leaving until I figure out what's going on with the
biotosis," Erik insisted.

"But what can you do?"

"I'll lie here, look at it, and think. And you, my friend, will
help me examine and analyze our sweet watery gelatin."

Sergei smiled and approached Erik.

"You're a pig, Eri. Maybe I'm not a real scientist. I find a mental leap more exciting than practical application. I've spent my life dreaming of working on a major project."

"A hundred million tons of polymer isn't enough for you?"

"That's not it. A hundred million tons of the biotosis or a hundred million tons of coal—the amount and materials are on the same level. And now unbelievable things are going on in the world. Think what the W-effect means!" Sergei paced the room excitedly. "Do you understand, even a little? Mutual psychic penetration! Telepathic gobbledygook in action! How, what, why? No one can answer these questions. Every scientist in the world is confused. Governments have been in session all week, trying to figure out how to deal with their citizens."

"Hold on," Erik said. "No one's gone mad yet, but it's true that very strange things have been observed. Why? I don't know, and right now, I don't care."

"Maybe you can explain why the strange things are seen all over the world, and you and I are not affected? Everything is the same as always for us. No telepathic effects, huh?"

"I can't answer that question, but the point isn't us, anyway. The doctor says that nothing in particular is happening in town, either. Almost—"

"But there is some effect, right?"

"Almost nothing. But that's not the point, either. The most important thing is to always know your place. If you can solve the riddle of EMO, then go there and do it. If not, then you're better off working on the biotosis. Well, what bright ideas do you have? How should we combat the W-effect?"

"I don't know. I just want to work on it."

"Well, wanting isn't enough. Look, it's almost evening. Time to do the photographs."

Sergei stomped off angrily. He rolled out the camera and dolly and got ready to start the filming. Erik watched through the window as Sergei deftly attached the automatic film-speed regulator to the camera, loaded the camera, turned it on.

"Sergei!"

Sergei came over to the window.

"You were wrong when you said there was no EMO here.

You told me yourself that on August 15, that night that I was hurt, you had some strange experiences. Remember? And the blood on your arm, when you gave me the shot—it could be related to the effect of mutual overlay."

"Maybe. But except for that night, nothing else strange happened to either of us."

"Yes. . . . Look at that beauty."

Erik pointed to the polymer mountain, or Biopeak #1, as they had named it. Sergei shook his head in a way that made it impossible to tell whether he was agreeing with Erik or condemning him for his weakness.

The biotosis really did look like a gigantic exotic flower. The sun's rays, reflected in the polished surface of its petals, filled the air with a flickering light. It was impossible to tell where the polymer ended and the delicate light-filled air began. Barely visible lines of red and blue, looking like zigzags of lightning, ran into the interior of the mass, where they formed a moving ball that constantly changed its shape. It looked as though some huge living thing was moving in the flower's body. But close inspection revealed that it was only the play of light and shadow. Erik could watch this play for days on end. He never tired of it. His whole being absorbed the dance of the lights and the bustle of color in the folds and creases of the biotosis. Its fine perfume seemed to him the sweetest in the world. Sergei merely snorted when Erik suggested that he breathe it in deeply. "A mixture of urine and cologne," he announced acidly. They were different people.

"Here's the doctor!" Sergei shouted.

Artem Ivanovich Karmin, the doctor, flew in every day from the neighboring town to see Erik. He examined Erik, gave him shots, prescribed new medications, and swore. But Erik stood firm: he would not leave until everything was clear.

"Hello, hermit crabs!" Karmin said as he jumped down from the running board of the aerocar. "When will you be scuttling off?" he asked, shaking Sergei's hand. Sergei motioned toward the window.

"Yes, I know," the doctor said and nodded sympathetically. "It's a difficult case, in every way."

They went into the house.

"What's new, Artem?" Erik asked.

"The world is full of news, it's buzzing away. But there is one bit of news especially for you, young man. If you agree to leave here—"

"Now, Artem, you know I can't be moved." Erik acted hurt.

"You couldn't be moved before, but now it's all right. Besides, we have a marvelous ambulance."

"Let's drop it, all right, doctor?"

"You're a stubborn ass. What am I supposed to do with you? Don't you realize that in Moscow the doctors are using EMO in their work? The doctor actually climbs into the skin of his patient, and he knows exactly what hurts and where. And then the doctor understands his patient. Diagnostic science has leaped forward, thanks to the W-effect. And I don't even have an X-ray of your bones. I don't know how they're knitting, what hurts you precisely."

"That's your news?" Sergei asked, carrying in a tray with bottles and opened cans.

"No, no, that's only the introduction."

They had a glass of the viscous liqueur.

"Nice stuff," Sergei said. "When I drink it, for some reason I think of Lola."

"I think of her when I'm in a good mood." Erik smiled.

"Terrific, that Lola," Sergei said.

"Marvelous," Erik agreed.

"Excuse me, but who are we talking about?" Karmin asked.

The friends looked at each other.

"Just someone," Sergei answered vaguely.

"Hm, I see," the doctor said. "Well, here's the news. Rational creatures from another stellar system have landed on earth. They're the ones who are causing the W-effect and all the other nonsense."

"Bull!" said Sergei. "That's the same old flying-saucer junk. Quite fashionable for a while, I remember."

"Don't jump to conclusions, young man. Our scientists have announced the spot where this cosmic intelligence might be found. Somewhere in the southern Pacific. Of course, they don't speak directly about space visitors, just about the source of psychic overlay, but it's easy to read between the lines. They've already sent out an exploratory expedition."

"So that's it," Sergei said slowly. "In the Pacific Ocean. It just doesn't reach us here. Well, did they find anything?"

"We don't know yet. It should be on the news soon."

"And do you believe in it, doctor?"

"Who knows? On the one hand, I guess not. But then, how do you explain all these miracles? When you give it some thought, you come to a similar conclusion. . . ." He changed the subject. "Well, how's your mound doing?"

Erik perked up. He had taken no part in the conversation until this point.

"Look close," Erik said.

The doctor stared into the darkness. There were pale lights, like fireflies, under the ashen surface of the biotosis. Just barely glimmering, they seemed to be in constant danger of going out But they didn't; in fact, they got stronger and stronger.

"We discovered this glow a long time ago, soon after it grew. It starts right after sundown. The intensity has been increasing every day," Erik said.

"Look! They're moving."

"Yes, they never stop. We've been recording it in slow motion. Sergei, bring the projector. Let's show the film to Artem. I'd like to see last night's film, too."

Sergei left the room. The doctor fiddled with the dials on the large radio in its blue plastic casing that stood in the corner of the room.

"What's the nature of this light?" he asked.

"Luminescence."

Sergei brought in the projector and the metal film cans. As he was setting up the equipment, he noticed that the doctor was listening intently to the foreign broadcast.

"You can understand it?"

"Yes, some of it. It's very interesting."

"Why don't you translate while I set this up."

The doctor bit his lip and began:

"It's from Italy. . . . They say that EMO has changed the entire life style of the country. . . . Normal relations between people have been destroyed. There are no more secrets. The hidden has become the visible. Lies are only possible at long distance, in letters or by phone.... Totally uneducated people can now be judges and doctors.... Those have become the easiest professions. I don't understand this part. ' 'oh, I see. The hardest profession now is business. Many companies have been bankrupted because of... they call it disclosure.... Oh, I get it, because of the disclosure of business secrets.... Ho-ho, it's getting rough for the capitalists.... Barodi, an important economist, has announced that the country must fight this devilish invasion. He said that the 'effect' has a definite communist leaning...."

"Just imagine, you can no longer fool other people while you shake hands and look them in the eye! How unfair!" Erik said, tearing himself away for a moment from the flickering screen.

"Yes, that's really tough," Sergei added.

"The members of parliament are demanding new working quarters. In keeping with the new conditions. They want to keep a certain distance from each other.... Reporters are accumulating hundreds of sensational stories. Unexpected revelations about members of the ruling party.... People are avoiding all contact.... Here's news from Africa. Yesterday near Lauria, the capital of Tam, fighting broke out between insurgents and government forces. Approximately fifty thousand people took part. This was the most amazing battle in the history of mankind, the ATI said. After the first shot, which felled Sergeant Maruss, all the combatants, including the prince's courtiers and the insurgents' general staff, rushed out onto the battlefield. Officers, soldiers, observers, and councilors hugged their enemies and cried. All arms were destroyed. Then the crowd marched on Lauria in tight formation. They were met by the inhabitants, who were ecstatically happy. The prince announced his abdication. Store owners are giving away their goods for free. People are not demanding wages for their labor. The city's vitality has reached an all-time peak. Our correspondent reports that he has never seen so many truly happy people anywhere. He reports that he is as infinitely happy as the residents of Tam. Life is free... they trust their neighbors... yet discipline and order are maintained.... People go to work, the plants and factories are producing.... We are led by some force...."

"Sergei, let me see the light calculator," Erik said quickly, turning on the pleasantly humming projector.

"Excuse me, when did all this happen there?" he asked the doctor.

"Somewhere around six P.M. Their time, of course. Why do you ask?"

"I just had a thought, and I'd like to check it out. Please hand me the atlas. It's on the top shelf."

"Yes, things are happening out there, while we sit here smelling the biotosis," Sergei grumbled.

"You can leave if you like, but I think those things out there will lead you right back here," Erik said, quickly flipping through the atlas.

"What are you trying to say?"

"Nothing for now, absolutely nothing."

Sergei yawned.

"I'll go get a sample of the biotosis for tomorrow."

"When did you take the last one?"

"I only took one. The day after Biopeak #1 grew. And I've run out. I'd better get some more, or I won't have anything to experiment on tomorrow."

He left. Erik smiled at Karmin's sympathetic look.

"He's bored. He thinks that if he started running up and down the street, he would find the explanation for the W-effect. If I were well, he would have left long ago. But I can't leave. The biotosis has turned out to be a tremendously interesting thing. It's not worth a thing as a polymer source, of course. Though, it might be useful. But . . . did you see the shining dots on its surface? I've been counting them and I've discovered an inexplicable regularity. Those dots—I call them swamp lights—are distributed unevenly. There are more in some places than in others. Sometimes they move, sometimes they're still. More often they move. Some die out, others light up. I've tabulated the number of dots in the different parts of the biotosis. And I've found an amazing repetition that I'm trying to figure out. There are several areas on the biotosis' surface where the number of swamp lights is the same. For example, if you find an accumulation of a hundred thousand dots in the lower layer, then you'll find the same accumulation in the middle layer, and the high middle layer, and the top layer."

"How many areas like that are there?"

"So far, I've found five, but that's not completely accurate, because there are several unclear transitional zones."

"How do you explain the existence of these local disturbances in the biotosis?"

"For now, I don't. I'm fascinated by the regularity of it all. And the lights, as I could tell from the photos, do vary. Some are brighter and more distinct, others are slightly weaker with vaguer outlines. The calculator works to an accuracy of plus or minus one. The lights travel in the most varied directions. As a rule, their movement is limited to the local area of disturbance, but sometimes they move from one accumulation to another. And there are lights outside these areas."

"That's interesting," Artem Ivanovich said slowly.

"And now," Erik continued excitedly, "I was just looking at yesterday's film of one part of the biotosis and I noticed.... Well, look for yourself."

The projector went on. It began to smell of hot film. Black flames jumped around on the screen.

"That's a general view," Erik explained when Karmin saw the glowing cone shape of the biotosis.

"And here's an area of magnification."

"But that's the sky, the sky with stars!" the doctor shouted.

"It really looks it, doesn't it? But that's only the biotosis, or the smelly jelly, as Sergei calls it."

Stars shimmered on the screen. Big and small, blindingly bright and barely glimmering, they rushed along convoluted curves, collided, disappeared, flared up again. Groups of stars separated from the central accumulation and rushed off in the dark field in various directions. New groups traveled toward them, joining them, and continued rushing with them as a new mass. Only close observation showed that for some of the time some of the stars stayed in place.

"A wonderful sight!"

"There, you see? And you wanted to take me away from this spectacle, which is as yet unsolved. Now notice this section. Here, in the top corner, there is an accumulation of one hundred and twelve thousand lights, according to the calculator. A new accumulation grew next to it last night. Do you see how new lights are converging on this spot from every direction?"

"Yes, I do. But—"

"Last night, when this film was taken, there were fifty-seven thousand of them. And then something happened. They melted into one very bright dot. Notice that there is no other star that bright on the biotosis. It's not a dot, it's a mass."

Karmin saw the glowing mass float upward.

"It's going to connect with the hundred-and-twelve-thousand-dot accumulation, see? And everything will change. All the separate far-flung lights are forming one huge spot, see? The individual centers of disturbance are being replaced by one common center!"

"Interesting," the doctor said, "but I don't quite see—"

"And now, what do you think?" Erik was practically shouting. "Why do you think I was digging around in the atlas? You give up? I was looking up the population of Lauria!"

Karmin gazed at the young man uncomprehendingly.

"What are you saying?"

"I. . . ." Erik stopped and fell back. Karmin rushed toward him. A bluish pallor came to Erik's cheeks. His nostrils were harshly outlined in blue.

"I must be overexcited. I don't feel well," Erik whispered.

The doctor picked up his hand and dropped it in horror. A searing pain burned his palm, like a lightning bolt. The lights went out in the room. The darkness was filled with scrambling sparks. Karmin had the sensation of flight. He was rushing headlong with dizzying speed, barely recognizing the vague outlines of houses and streets. He grabbed things as he went past, and they turned out to be cold rock with a porous surface, or a smooth handle, or soft human flesh. Suddenly his violent race ended. The first thing he felt were the heavy rubber boots over his knees. They were filled with water. Water was splashing quietly at his feet, dripping from the dark anthracite ceiling, seeping from all the cracks in the walls. It was hot in the mine. The miner's lamp in his helmet shone dully. Karmin knew that he was in a collapsed mine shaft and had been there for several hours. There was no hope of rescue. With dull despair, wiping the beads of sweat from his brow, he examined the heavy pieces of coal that blocked the exit. Women's faces rose in his imagination. One was a full round face, under a cap of blond curls, connected for some reason with the name Elsa. The other was a coquettish face with lively black eyes. Her name was Joan, and he had known that for a long time. But he could not guess why she was there. He waved his hand, trying to wave them away, and got up and went over to the rubble. The collapsed roof had left a mound of large rocks and soft dust that had turned to mud.

"They won't be here in time," he muttered, and he was surprised to hear that he wasn't speaking Russian. But not too surprised. Splashing in his boots through the black water, he slowly dragged several boulders into the corner. He moved the medium and small pieces of coal there, too—the fruits of an hour's labor. Working feverishly, he cleared the front of the area in a few minutes. It was hard to breathe; the hot air seemed to be permeated with humidity. He undressed, leaving only his helmet with the light, and went back to the landslide. Everything that he pulled out of the rubble he dragged over to the side and piled up into a neat wall. A gap was slowly forming, but he was suffocating. He had to sit down on a wet rock and catch his breath. The water was up to his knees now. He stared in horror at its dirty surface, with dust and fragments of coal floating in it. Then he got up and went back to the pile. He worked methodically and calmly. He thought that the pile wasn't so big and that he would be able to get out into the main shaft. That had probably collapsed, too, but that wasn't so bad. The important thing was that there would be air there, and the water wouldn't be rising so fast. He hoped to sit it out in one of the bends in the shaft. He would be able to wait even a whole day until help came.

He glanced up from time to time at the cracked ceiling that looked like a gutted shark's belly. The crack gaped at him. He worked carefully, afraid of disturbing the death that hung over him. Once in a while he would touch the jagged edges of the opening tenderly and softly, as if it were a woman's face. His trembling fingers barely touched the damp glistening layers of coal. He wanted to test the security of the ceiling, but he was afraid of another cave-in.

He had made his way several yards into the rubble when water rushed in from above. Its force knocked him down, and he fell flat on his back. He looked up and waited for the ceiling to collapse. But it held. Several rocks were dislodged by the water, and one hit him in the face. It struck his nose and temple, and he lost consciousness. The cave-in, the black walls, the burbling water, the yellow lamplight dissolved in the dark....

Sergei opened the door wide. Hesitating at the threshold, he spoke:

"Erik, I couldn't take a sample. I'll be damned if I know why, but I couldn't."

No one answered. There was chaos in the room. All the furniture was piled up against one wall, including Erik's supports. Karmin lay under the window, spread-eagled. Sergei bent over him. There were large beads of sweat on the doctor's face and his open eyes stared unseeing beyond Sergei.

"Artem! Doctor!" Sergei called.

Karmin said nothing.

"Erik? What happened?" Erik lay in his litter staring at a spot on the ceiling. His face contorted and he screamed. A grimace of pain crossed his face. Sergei saw a dark stripe travel across his forehead. It was blue, then purple, and then, tearing in a few spots, it bled red. Erik moaned and looked at Sergei. His pupils were enormously dilated. Karmin sat up under the window. Sergei turned and saw that his face was cut in the same way as Erik's.

"What happened here?"

Karmin crossed the room and checked Erik's pulse.

"What happened?" He repeated Sergei's question, examining his own blistered hand. "I am convinced of the presence of space visitors on our planet. A powerful intelligence has come to us, and it can do what it wants with us."

"I disagree," Erik whispered, barely able to move his lips.

Chapter 5

"I DON'T WANT to let you go," said Ermolov, setting aside Kara-bichev's request. "I have good reasons. We need you here. The government is undertaking extraordinary measures to discover the causes of EMO. An entire army of scientists has been mobilized to deal with the problem."

"With no results as yet," Karabichev noted.

"The problem is too complex. We are unarmed. That damned radiation cannot be recorded by any known apparatus."

"Except man."

"Yes. But nevertheless, we shouldn't lose confidence. We'll find the source of the radiation. And for that we need specialists like you."

"I can't," Karabichev said softly, staring fixedly at nothing. "And besides, why is it necessary to work right here? The phenomenon can be studied at any point of the globe. During my trip, I'll be able to—"

"—to do nothing," Ermolov interrupted. "Secondly, what is there in that letter, anyway? It's lunatic raving. Nothing concrete."

"We're all raving nowadays."

"You don't even know where to look for her. You can't tell anything from the postmark. A letter can be mailed from anywhere. And she herself writes that you shouldn't come now. Take my advice, put it off for a while."

"I can't. I know that she's in trouble. She could die."

"And what about your Maria here in Moscow?"

Karabichev looked glum.

"I've decided to turn her over to your care," he said. "She is an interesting specimen of almost total psychic transmutation, and our institute should get involved in her case."

"Hm."

"Her face and voice have changed. She doesn't look like my Maria any more."

"Makeup, diet?"

"Diet? Well, yes, she has lost weight. But that's not it. She's a stranger to me. Her personality, her habits, the way she moves. In a word, it's bad."

"Yes."

Ermolov thought, raised his eyebrows, and spoke.

"Yes, you're in a fix. All right. So you've decided to go? You insist?"

"Yes. You're going to have to send someone to Cape Horn. So send me. I won't stay in Bessano long. The *Languedoc* sails from Marseilles to Buenos Aires on the eleventh. I've checked."

"Well, all right then. Do what you think is best. I still think it's all a lot of nonsense. You should sit in Moscow and wait for things to change. But your idea about checking out Cape Horn is a good one. Do you at least know the language?"

"Tolerably."

"Mmm. All right. Fine. But make sure you're in Marseilles on the eleventh."

"Of course. And in Buenos Aires on the twenty-second and on Cape Horn on the twenty-fifth."

When Karabichev landed in the port of Bessano, it was early morning. The sun played on the sidewalks, heavily sprinkled with fish scales. A red-faced giant grabbed his bags and loped up the steps that led to the city; Karabichev barely managed to keep up with him. He heard the jabber of the dock workers, the whine of the cranes, and the roar of motors. The unnaturally bright colors of the south blinded him. At times he could sense other souls, hot and heavy like heated irons.

The porter brought him out onto an empty street planted with myrtle. Large stray dogs and small dirty children wandered along the dusty cobblestones. The morning air was heating up. He could hear the clatter of dishes, cries, and laughter coming through the thin screens in the open windows. Someone was playing a guitar, humming to himself. A woman was screaming coarse curses at someone. A car, an exhibit from a historical museum, drove down the street.

They stopped at the hotel. The small two-story house was overgrown with ivy and surrounded by so many trees that it looked like a green grotto. Karabichev paid the giant and he left, his head in its torn dirty cap held high.

Only now, when he looked out onto the roofs of the city from his hotel window, did Karabichev understand the magnitude of his problem. To find Maria in this big city, knowing nothing about her, would not be easy. Taking one last look at the skinny and fat red chimneys floating in the hazy air, he sighed and sat at the table. He took out the letter and pored over it one more time. Maria had written:

"...something absolutely horrible has befallen me. I'm ashamed and it's hard to write about it, I still can't believe it. I think, I'm almost positive, that it's related to the appearance of the space visitors that everybody's talking about. My situation is terrible, and the only thing that saves me is my faith that it will not last. I want to see you and I can't, not in this condition. That's why I ask you not to look for me. Don't spend your strength and health. You can't help me anyway. We can only hope and wait. I would never have risked writing to you if I didn't have hope. . . ."

Karabichev folded the paper and put it in his pocket. He ate the breakfast brought by a waiter and left the hotel.

Karabichev strolled around the unfamiliar city. Everything seemed extraordinarily new and yet somehow familiar. The center of Bessano was cleaner than the waterfront section. But within thirty yards of his hotel, Karabichev came across a beggar sitting on the sidewalk. The legless man handed him a dirty note. Karabichev could not make out the words scribbled on the paper and hastily tossed a coin into the aluminum cup. The cripple followed him with his deep dark eyes.

Men and women hurried past Karabichev. People went into stores and walked out of them, parked their aerocars, laughed, and sometimes argued. The soft local babble irritated Karabichev and he found the extravagant gestures of the inhabitants theatrical. And it was only when he fell into the sphere of a passerby that Karabichev realized that they were just like himself.

Soon he found himself in front of a house that had too much glass and clear plastic. And the metal and concrete that had gone into the fence would have been enough to build a small factory. They did not like greenery here: a scrawny cactus grew in the sand in the front yard. Karabichev rang the bell and was with the host a few minutes later. He handed him a letter of recommendation from a famous Soviet scientist. Karabichev looked at Señor Rioli while he deciphered the scrawl. Sleek, thin, and wise. With a light gesture of his hand, his host offered Karabichev a drink of dark-red liqueur in a tall decanter. Karabichev politely sipped the cool liquid. Señor Rioli spoke. His angular face became animated with welcoming wrinkles. He interjected Russian words into his speech. Karabichev had little trouble understanding him.

"Lakhutin asks me to cooperate with you. But in what? The letter is not clear. Would you be so kind as to explain?"

Karabichev explained.

"There are three hundred thousand inhabitants in Bessano," Rioli said, "and a hundred and eighty thousand of them are women. You understand. . . ."

Rioli had the habit of not finishing his sentences. The inter-locutor was expected to do that. But Karabichev said nothing, and the professor went on:

"Of course, we can advertise in the papers and on the radio. The city administration will help us. These are such difficult times that. . . ."

"I would rather not attract the attention of the press."

Rioli looked up in surprise.

"You see, she would be against it. She didn't want us to meet right now."

The professor pressed his lips together.

"Then it's much more difficult than I had thought. Well, we won't make any decisions for now. Get to know the city, live here a bit, and then, maybe, we'll think of something. I'll be your guide and helper in my free time. We have an extremely difficult mission, you understand that yourself."

The days after his initial conversation with Rioli were filled with fruitless search and disillusionment. Consultations with the police led to nothing. "You're just wasting your time, Señor Karabichev," the mayor told him, spreading his plump hands. "If your wife does not wish to respond, no one can help you." Rioli would rub his nose and tell him not to give up. And Kara-bichev didn't. Every morning he would leave his hotel, toss a coin to the legless beggar, and set off on his search. He spent the whole day wandering through the smoky lavender city, ask-ing questions. People would answer with a smile and a shrug. Karabichev got to know Bessano well. The clean, proper center of town had its expensive blocks, where children played in shady fenced-in gardens. The commercial section was lively at any time of day or night, lit up in multicolored neon. The dank dock area contained warehouses, factories, and masses of hard-working people.

He was recognized on the street by now. Some people nodded hello. His knowledge of Spanish did not help him very much. A strange mixture of Spanish and Portuguese was spoken in Bes-sano, and the many generations of Bessanese seamen had added salty words and curses from every language of the world. If it weren't for the possibility of understanding people without words,

Karabichev would have given up long ago. He could only talk to Rioli, who spoke a cultured, literary language.

"As you see," the professor said, "the appearance of the W-effect on earth has some positive aspects."

They were sitting in an open café, from which they could see down to the port and the dark sea. Rioli had just come back from the suburbs, where his institute was located. He was wearing a suit made of a mat fabric that automatically regulated the temperature, like an air conditioner.

"By the way, speaking of space creatures," he said, "the expedition returned from the Pacific with no results at all. The area indicated by your scientists and by the Americans is completely uninhabited. There's nothing and no one there."

"Is that so?" Karabichev's eyes lighted up. The topic was a scientific one, and therefore interesting.

"Yes," said Rioli, waving his arms. He seemed to be quite pleased by the expedition's failure. "So, of course, they immediately came up with new explanations. Carlos Carlos maintains that our galactic neighbors are sitting on the ocean floor and pulling their tricks on us underwater. A depth of two hundred and fifty fathoms is supposedly a mere piffle to them. That may very well be, but it may not. Only one thing is clear: the world has changed and is constantly changing as a result of the W-effect."

Rioli smiled. A waiter glided past. The sea darkened on the horizon. Yellow lights came on. The people walking past the café were no longer hurrying. Music that had been drowned out by the day's bustle sounded throughout the street. Flowers had a stronger scent. Women's heels clicked louder. The bright light of day turned into deep-violet twilight.

"Let's take a walk," Karabichev suggested.

The mysterious approach of evening made him sad. A vague idea was troubling him.

"With pleasure," Rioli replied.

They left the café, maintaining the "distance of politeness," the distance that kept people free from the effect. Walking with Rioli, Karabichev had often wanted to get closer, to check his intuitions about the professor. But something stopped him.

"And I feel," Rioli said heartily as they walked, "that there is no point in looking for the visitors from outer space."

"Why not?"

"For many reasons. First of all, no one can find them, and second, they shouldn't be found."

"I don't understand."

"I will explain, if you wish. By the way, that beautiful woman you're watching has no relation to your wife. She works in the men's department of one of our stores."

Karabichev nodded. "Yes, yes, I'm all ears," he said and sighed.

"What is wrong with Carlos Carlos' theories?" Rioli asked, cutting through the dark spicy air with his walking stick. "They assume too much. The spacemen can live under water, they can float around like microbes in the air, they can make themselves invisible—all these theories have been propounded. But where are the spacemen? Who has recorded their presence? If they are material, they should show up under a microscope, or in a transmitter, or in a chemist's test tube, or in a physicist's apparatus. But so far no one's caught anything. Not a single piece of equipment and not a single human eye has seen them. There is nothing except a strange malady, called the W-effect. But it is all inside people, not outside them. And that's why I say that there are no visitors from outer space here, there are no rational beings living under the Pacific Ocean or running around invisible through the air. They do not exist, do you understand?"

Rioli stopped, turned, and stared into Karabichev's eyes.

"All right. Then what is it?" Karabichev asked impatiently.

"So, there is no one but man on earth. We're speaking naturally of rational creatures. All right. Then what? Why? And so on.... You see, I have a very simple idea of the appearance of the W-effect. Let us review a few episodes in evolution. The proto-sea of life. The soup in which protein was cooked up. Lumps of jelly, capable of metabolism. I'm just hitting the highlights, you understand. Proto-coacervates, coacervates, the first cell, an association of cells ... stop! Now here's the watershed. From cell to organism. From a unit to a multiplicity. From primitive solitude to specialized existence! It's advantageous! You see? Advantageous from nature's point of view. And whatever is to nature's advantage becomes law. And so it happened that the solitary helpless proto-coacervate, which had to do everything itself—digest food, react to light and sound and the presence of poisonous materials—became a powerful mobile association, which could have specialized tissues and cells, which had a developed form of locomotion, which had a regulated metabolism. It was to nature's advantage to unite separate cells into a powerful, living organism, and so it happened. The ever-developing and self-perfecting tree of evolution grew, and those associations of cells formed many branches, and man, as he himself maintains, crowned the tree. As far as I know, he didn't check with nature on that."

"All right. Go on," Karabichev said. Rioli's theories at least kept him from thinking about his personal problems.

"There it is. How do you go on? Has nature put an end to the tree of evolution? Have we stopped developing? It looks as though our organs are not changing. There are no new forms of people cropping up. We are becoming weaker and more delicate. And the animal world isn't creating new forms either. Does that mean that the tree will wither?"

"But—"

"Wait. I'm almost through. The ironclad law of biology states that whatever does not change, physically, fundamentally, dies. Man is not changing materially. For millennia he has remained the same, despite his scientific and technological progress. Following this biological logic, we must conclude that man, yes, man, as a unit of living matter, is doomed to extinction. But nature is kind and merciful. Its resources are limitless. It hints at the path to salvation. Even if man, per se, as a certain biological unit, is dying out, then society as a whole is progressing and developing. But human society has not become a unified organism. It is a mound of raw material from which the Great Man will be sculpted. And nature is building up to him, to the Great Man. Your communism—it's an attempt to create an organism from separate individuals—"

"Professor, what a way to see a communist society! First of all, it's not an organism, and—"

"Forgive me, Andrei, I did not mean to get political in the least. Anyway, it's nature that is seeking!

"What gets in the way? Lack of understanding. Language is an imperfect means of communication. It cannot express a millionth part of our mental states, and people remain misunderstood. Cheated, they retreat into themselves, and mistrust, envy, and dishonesty arise—the sins of contemporary civilization.

"For mankind to be united, there is a need for a new method of communication. And here it is—the overlay effect, or EMO. How? I don't know. But space has nothing to do with it. I think it's a question of evolution. Man has reached that stage of development when the emergence of a mutually affecting radiation is possible. It is characteristic of all people, regardless of age, sex, intelligence, nationality.

"That's why I say it can't be found. We'll never find it, because we're looking outside ourselves, and it's definitely within us."

"In other words," Karabichev interrupted, "you feel that people should be united in one huge organism, the Great Man, the way proto-cells once became the first multicellular organism?"

"That's about it."

"But that's a lot of nonsense, professor! Man is not a cell, and he can never be one. When you speak of the communists' desire to create such an organism, you mock us! You predict the total annihilation of the individual. I assure you that I have no desire to be the Great Man's earlobe. No one in my country would want to be. We are people, and we believe in free man in a free communist world."

"Ay-ay-ay!" Rioli shook his head. "What temperament! What mental energy! But a total absence of logic and self-criticism. Don't be angry. You've been a cell with a clearly defined specialty for a long time. You're a scientist? That means you're no earlobe. You are a piece of a brain wrinkle of the future Great Man. Tell me, do you feel any better knowing that? After all, specialization and differentiation are separating the members of human society more and more. The rich man doesn't understand the poor man, the worker his boss, the doctor the engineer, the judge the economist, the artist the mathematician, the farmer the laborer. People are separated, scattered, isolated. And what will unite them?"

"We have an idea to unite us. Communism."

"That's what you have. We don't. Our society is the future

Great Man's arms, and legs, and eyes. They have to be collected
and formed into an organism so that it will function. I feel that
the W-effect is the first stage in the synthesis of the Great Man.
First, total mutual understanding, and the melding of all people
into a single, common system." Karabichev snorted. Rioli got
angry. "Do you know that the USSR is being accused of ex-
panding its ideas with the help of this new type of radiation? No
matter what the Vatican may say about the Second Coming, the
W-effect works primarily for the benefit of the communists. In
Bessano alone, some twenty big companies went bankrupt because of the effect. And what's wrong with that? You shouldn't
picture the future Great Man on too primitive a scale. Of course,
people aren't exactly cells, and they won't grow together, even
though greater physical proximity isn't ruled out. Imagine the
moment when the world population reaches tens and hundreds
of billions. Then people will be like sardines in cans. There'll be
nowhere to go to escape man."

"There are other planets and other worlds."

"Nonsense! The same thing will happen there. Our talents in
that area are well proved. No, Señor Karabichev, no matter what
you say, we must unite. Not only the proletariat, but everybody,
regardless of his status, and unite not just ideologically, but
physically, too. An organism must be created, a new society, the
Great Man's brain, because their places will immediately be taken
People are closely tied to each other. The society is a living
creature made up of several billion cells, and each cell is a
human being. What is the place of governments in such a
soicety? Government, administration, regulation—the cybernetic
functions of the nervous system. That is, the brain. In fact, governments function as the brain in our present-day society. Not
always successfully, however. In the Great Man, it will be different. There will be many fewer rulers, and they will be so tightly
tied with each man individually that any change in the condition
of a single individual will immediately be felt in the nervous
system of the gigantic organism. And I might add that there will
be no passive, indifferent, and self-interested cell left in the
Great Man's brain, because their places will immediately be taken
by their active, conscientious neighbors. The dream of the people will come true: the rulers will experience on their own skins

the pain and difficulty of the people's life. The death penalty for
a member of the society will then be an amputation of their
own living flesh. War—a stupid suicide. Violence—another
pointless kind of self-destruction."

"An amazing picture! A nightmare I wouldn't want to see in
my sleep! That's a dictatorship worse than fascism!"

"Nothing of the kind. If you allow for the mobility of cells—
that is, moving from one function to another—and you—"

"How can I allow for that? You just got through telling me
about each cell's narrow specialization and concrete solidity in
one specific place. Can an intestinal cell become a cell on the
retina?"

"In the Great Man, yes," Rioli said firmly.

"Well, then . . . you're creating him out of unreal material."

"Why? There are no irreplaceable people on earth."

"That's not true. There are."

They argued for a long time, wandering about the streets of
nocturnal Bessano.

The air began to smell of the sea and of rotting fish; they had
reached the docks.

"Perhaps I'm wrong, or more precisely, not completely right,"
Rioli said. "My outline is vague and imprecise, and I'm doubt-
less wrong about a lot of things, but I believe firmly in one
thing."

Karabichev looked attentively at the wrinkled forehead and
the wise, dark, burning eyes.

"I believe in the limitless and constant development of nature,
particularly the evolution of the living world. I do not agree
that man is the crown of creation. People who say that place a
dunce cap on nature, not a crown on man. I believe that nature
will not stop with man and will go further. It is inevitable: no
radical changes are taking place in the human organism. The
next source of man's power is in society. Evolution is gradually
bringing man to creating a new form of social order. Your communism is powerful because it has anticipated a future stage of
evolution. And its just and comforting aspects, which you bring
up so often, have nothing to do with it. Your ideas capture the
minds of men because they anticipate the future accurately.
Anticipation of the future—that is the strength of any concept

in science. But you shouldn't stop halfway. The Great Man must be created by nature. And the W-effect is the first swallow of spring. By the way, I've sent my ideas on evolution and mutual psychic overlay to the United Council on Studying the W-effect."

Karabichev could only shrug. Everything was logical in Rioli's argument, but it was inhuman in its generalizations and deductions. It would be hard to convince him of any other point of view; he was insulated by his conservative stubbornness as a major scholar and the prejudices arising from his ideology.

They were walking down a poorly lit sidestreet. Flashes of light and snatches of conversation spilled out onto the street from the partially opened doors. They could hear castanets and heartrending songs. Women hid in the leafy shadows under the trees. Someone was crying behind a fence. Karabichev felt an inexplicable anxiety; he wanted to determine where it was coming from, but Rioli interfered with that. The professor loped along the sidewalk, raising his legs high like a stork, and kept talking and talking.

There was a small crowd at the corner. A man in a cassock was haranguing the crowd, raising his hands to the heavens, then pressing them to his thin, flat chest, which supported a large silver cross. He was shouting and rushing his words, and Karabichev couldn't understand him. Rioli listened for a while and grinned.

"He's predicting the Second Coming."

Karabichev laughed

"You see, there's another explanation of the W-effect."

They walked a few more steps and stopped, attracted by a strange scene. A group of loiterers had gathered under an awning. A man was crawling around on a carpet in the harsh rusty light of the streetlamp. His naked black chest glistened dully. His head was thrown back and swaying gently in rhythm with his hoarse speech. His black eyes searched the crowd, seeing nothing, understanding nothing. He would jump up once in a while, hands outstretched, barking out words that must have been orders and commands. The crowd laughed.

"That is a completely normal man," Rioli said. "Healthy, smart . . . I know him. But EMO's bitter cup did not pass him by. His body is here, but he is receiving his sensory input from somewhere in India. He works there as an elephant handler. He can hear our voices, but simultaneously he hears those with whom he works. He sees us and he sees his elephants, the forests, a river. And the second set of inputs is much stronger. Basically, he lives there, not here. His neighbors and people with nothing to do come around to watch him and have a laugh. He constantly describes what's happening to him."

"There's another argument against your society-organism. And that's only the beginning," Karabichev said.

Rioli and Karabichev walked on in silence. The streets were getting darker and narrower, and they saw fewer people. The ones they did encounter were pathetic-looking, or worse, downright suspicious. The men hid in the shadows, and their voices rumbled threateningly from the darkness. The women tried to call attention to themselves. Their naked desire to display the remains of faded beauty gave Karabichev a horrible thought. He realized that it had been brewing in his mind all evening. He turned to Rioli.

"Tell me, are there many brothels in Bessano?"

The professor, who had been raising and lowering his thin legs methodically, stopped short, as though up against a wall.

"I don't understand what . . ." he said, staring at Karabichev in surprise.

Karabichev said nothing.

"You think that she's in one?"

That was it, the answer! At first, a man lives with only a foreboding of it, and then it appears suddenly, and everything falls into place. Loose ends are tied up, hints and allusions are clarified, and the conclusion amazes us with its obviousness. "Ah, what a fool I was for not seeing it sooner! Maybe I'm wrong? No, too much is explained by it, too much."

Rioli hesitated and then said officiously:

"I cannot accompany you in this risky undertaking. My reputation. . . ."

"I'm not asking such a sacrifice from you, Señor Rioli. But could you at least show me. . . ."

Rioli looked around.

"We've gone so far! I don't know this area at all! Let's go back into midtown," he said.

They walked hurriedly from the dark, smelly dockside streets.

"I live right here!" Karabichev cried.

"Well, then you won't have far to go to return." Rioli grinned as they shook hands.

The professor went off. Karabichev looked around the square. Lone figures occasionally crossed its dark-gray pentagonal surface. It was late, and the neon lights were going out one after another.

It was very close to the hotel, and Karabichev thought how good it would be to get back to his room and leaf through the *Voice of Bessano*.

He felt that he was being watched. He looked around and saw no one. On the right, under the lights of the closed café, there was a sack left out on the sidewalk. Karabichev got close to the sack, and felt that it was watching him, looking straight into his eyes. Before he realized what was happening, the "sack" stirred and rolled off with a curse, pushing off from the pavement with its hands. It was the beggar. He recognized Karabichev now, and gladly took his coins, but crawled away cursing every time. Perhaps he did not like Karabichev's foreign looks, which set him off from the rest of Bessano's inhabitants? Most likely, he was just a poorly brought-up beggar.

Karabichev crossed the square and turned down one of the five streets that converged on it. He stopped in front of the house Rioli had pointed out. He gave one last look at the twisting street and rang the doorbell. He had the impression that a shadow was creeping along the street. He wanted to look at it directly, but the door opened and he went into the house.

There were three men in the brightly lit parlor, lazily leafing through albums with brass clasps. There was a counter in the back of the room, and the madam was behind it. Stuttering and blushing, Karabichev explained his reason for being there. The madam raised her black, leechlike eyebrows.

"A Russian? Maria? No, there's been no one like that. I understand, I understand everything. But not one of my girls said she felt like that. They have different . . . feelings. But not one has said she's become a Russian. That hasn't happened. But you can ask them yourself, if you like. Some are free—"

Karabichev quickly refused and shot out of the door. He felt steadier in the fresh air. "Not too cool in these situations, eh?" he thought to himself and smiled.

But he couldn't stop halfway. He had to find out one way or the other. And so he went to the next house, which was only a few yards away. He had the impression again that he was being followed by a shadow. He looked back. The movement and rustle behind him stopped. Karabichev decided to ignore it.

He wasn't exactly welcomed at the second house. He had to climb up to the third floor. Half-dressed men and women scurried back and forth in the long, dim hallway. No one could understand Karabichev's questions, and he was ready to bolt when the owner of the business showed up. The diminutive and neatly coiffed man was amused by Karabichev's request. He found the situation immensely funny.

"Your wife? Your wife?" he repeated several times. "Sorry, but unfortunately nothing like that's happened here," he said, smoothing his waxed mustache.

Fortunately, you son of a bitch, fortunately for you, Karabichev thought as he tipped his hat.

As he was leaving he witnessed a disgusting spectacle. Some drunken animal was beating a girl on the stairs. Her head was tossed back over the railing. She did not resist, but screamed once in a while. Her long hair was caught in the painted latticework.

Without even thinking, Karabichev pushed the drunkard away. He fell down the stairs. Karabichev helped the girl up. She was unbelievably emaciated and pathetic. Half her face was covered with two huge bruises. Mumbling servile words of thanks, the girl disappeared. Karabichev looked around. The battlefield was clear. The enemy had fled. Not a single door had opened during the incident. Obviously, this was a common occurrence in this part of the world. Karabichev sighed, cursed the social system that led to such evil, and went downstairs.

He left the house and stopped indecisively at the corner. Which way? A man came out of the shadows of the house nearby and headed straight for him. Karabichev shuddered and froze. He felt several short painful jabs in his right side. His assailant smelled of stale alcohol and rotting fish. Karabichev fell, and as he fell, he heard a scream. The drunkard who had attacked him was screaming. Karabichev saw him drop his knife, grab his side, and fall on the sidewalk next to him. Karabichev closed his eyes. He wasn't surprised by what he had just seen. Nothing surprised him any more.

Maria's voice penetrated his fog.

"Andrei, Andrei, are you alive, my darling?" But her voice sounded harsh and strange. He opened his eyes. There was no Maria there, of course. The drunkard was flat on his back nearby. The legless beggar was leaning over him. Tears were streaming down his wrinkled, stubbly cheeks. Karabichev watched in horror as the beggar's thick cracked lips moved and formed the words:

"Andrei, Andrei."

"No, no, not that, please, not that!" Karabichev shouted and passed out.

Señor Rioli struggled out of sleep. The videophone sounded as though it would burst from excitement. The signal lights flashed on and off. The bell clamored. Stifling a yawn, the professor turned the phone on.

A few minutes' conversation with the police chief made it clear that Karabichev was in trouble. Of course, yes, he knew the foreigner. Yes, the letter of recommendation was addressed to him. It wasn't a forgery. Yes, he would be right over.

"The strangest part of it all, professor," the medical examiner was saying, "is that it's not at all clear who attacked whom. Your protégé has three knife wounds in the right side, not fatal, but bad enough. The bandit who attacked him died of severe shock. And he complained of terrible pain in the right side, in the same places where the Russian was wounded. The autopsy showed that the deceased had formed clots in the liver area that blocked the veins. By wounding another, he killed himself."

"Why does that surprise you?" Rioli asked. "We've seen a lot like it. How many cases have there been where assailants felt all the pain of their victims? The bandit struck several times, fell under the W-effect, and felt the wounds in his own side. Probably his liver was in bad shape anyway, and his nervous system convulsed, bringing on shock and death. If he had knifed his victim in the back or some other place, he probably would have survived. Just some pain."

"We live in just times," the examiner joked.

"Precisely. And justice is becoming palpable. You can feel it with your hands."

"Or in your side?"

"Possibly."

Rioli went into the hospital room. Karabichev's eyes were shut and had dark circles under them. He was breathing heavily and muttering. The professor listened. He was talking about his wife, Maria, about some legless beggar in St. Sebastian's Square, and other nonsense. Karabichev was blaming himself for some mistake, couldn't forgive himself for something.

Rioli left the hospital. It was morning. Warm and happy light was pouring into the streets. The sky was clear and the air fresh. Rioli sighed.

"Everything will be all right. Justice and evolution will prevail."

Suddenly he saw a human stump huddling under the hospital wall. Was that the beggar of Karabichev's ravings?

"Hey you, come here," he said, beckoning for the beggar to come closer.

Bowing and scraping and thanking the "kind señor," the beggar rolled up to the professor.

"Do you know Señor Karabichev?" he asked. The beggar looked at him in puzzlement and said:

"Carabiccio?"

"Yes."

His cheek twitched and pathetic bitter tears ran down his cheeks. He turned away and his figure became even smaller, as though he had been pushed into the ground. He parted the branches of the bushy oleanders and disappeared in their blue-black shadows.

"Andrei, Andrei!" It sounded like a weak sigh.

Rioli squeezed his eyes shut and rubbed his hand under his eyes, as though brushing away cobwebs.

The fresh bright sun was getting hot. The blinding white-washed walls still retained the night's dampness. They seemed blue. A dirty pigeon pecked at a cigarette stub.

Professor Rioli was going home.

The street to Via Grasso was closed, and the driver turned down a narrow sidestreet. It reeked of fried mackerel and olive oil. His nostrils were tickled by the smoke from outdoor grills. The lines of wash alternating with bands of pure blue made the sky look like a sailor's striped shirt.

The car meandered along the narrow dark streets. Finally it came out on a wide street.

An old open trolley rattled and swayed like a sailor in an unfamiliar port. Rioli had never been in this neighborhood. He looked through the window with great interest. He was not surprised to see a crowd at the end of the street. Everything seemed unsteady and unreal. He opened the window. The smell of rotting vegetables overwhelmed the other smells. The street noises grew in volume: cars, children's cries, women's arguments. Gradually, the crowd's rumble grew against the steady din of the street.

And then Rioli realized what was strange about the crowd. It was the crowd itself. Rioli realized with amazement that this was the first time he had seen so many people standing that close together.

"Are things back to the way they were before?" thought Rioli. "No more W-effect? We can visit friends without fear?"

He could see the faces of the oncoming crowd through the windshield. They were calm and intense. Dirty overalls, stained jeans, bright kerchiefs, large berets, shiny black hair. The crowd took over the entire street from sidewalk to sidewalk. The trolley was stopped. Its passengers were leaning out the windows that had never known glass. The conductor sat on the steps, eating bread with olives. Rioli's driver stopped the car, too, and got out. The professor stayed in the car. The crowd parted and came together again on the other side of the car, like a large quiet river that carefully goes around rocks but angrily brings down dikes, its cold waters swirling and bubbling. It seemed to encircle Rioli and carry him off. He whirled in its eddies and slowly melted into the current.

In the time it took the muscular, tanned people to walk by, shoulder to shoulder, Rioli understood everything. He became each of them and all of them. He was one with their work and their power. He felt—felt, because he had always known—their pitiful dark hovels, the squalling unwashed children, the damp heat of a coin held tightly in a fist. Your last coin.

Huge grotesque scenes flashed before him. Long lines in front of the unemployment offices, cities built out of packing crates, the forbidding silent factory gates, closed-down docks. Machinery, shovels, garbage heaps, cranes, gangplanks bending under the weight of dockworkers—everything rushed past him, seeping through his heart and brain.

The workers went on. Rioli was himself again. But he no longer had the sense of unity and strength that had filled him completely just a minute ago. Rioli sought the right word for it for a long time, but couldn't come up with it. The trolley bell clanged. The conductor wrapped his olives in a newspaper. Rioli's driver got back behind the wheel.

"They're okay, eh, señor?"

Rioli did not reply. He was still looking for the right word. It came to him by itself, falling into place.

"Solidarity," Rioli said unexpectedly.

"That's right, señor. It'll soon stop. People will be able to live in peace."

"I'm not talking about that. I mean solidarity."

"So do I, señor!"

Rioli realized that no W-effect or any other effect could separate those people. Or bring them any closer, either.

Evolution and revolution are the same process, thought Rioli and shuddered. It felt as though Karabichev had spoken those words inside him.

The car pulled out onto the highway. The air was filled with the scent of magnolias, lemon blossoms, and myrtle. As usual, the sea appeared unexpectedly. It languished in the silvery luxury of the thin sun, shimmering in the blue.

The white surf delineated the shore. There were few bathers. The gray and black pebbles looked cool and damp.

Rioli recalled the poet's lines: "So that all the rivers will finally fall into the sea...."

Chapter 6

THIS WASN'T THE FIRST TIME that Ruzhena had noticed a pale strip of light under the door of Sergei Arefyev's room as she was going home. One time she had stopped and listened. She thought she could hear a quiet buzzing.

Ruzhena went downstairs, got the keys, and returned to open the door to Sergei's room. I was right, someone's in here, she thought as she went in. A diffuse pink light fell on the dusty floor, but the lab was empty. The light was coming from the brain-wave concentrator, which Sergei had pushed into a far corner. The other equipment lay in a dead heap on the dark counters. Strange, she thought. Who turned it on?

The young woman moved the apparatus out into the middle of the room and fiddled with the regulator. Both the large and

the small rays intensified. The buzz turned into a joyous hum.
But it's working without electricity, Ruzhena realized as she saw
the plug on the floor. The thought gave her the creeps. She
played with the handle on the shiny control panel, and the pale
rays became a wide beam of lemon light. The humming stopped.
Music, tender, sad, and remote, filled the room. The sound of
someone very lonely singing about an unknown world. She stood
on tiptoe and looked into the concentrator. . . .

A feeling of profound satisfaction and happiness overcame
her. Her body became as light as air, almost weightless.

She sank into a chair, turning her face and chest into the
yellow rays coming from the reflector.

"How good it is," she muttered.

Gradually the room, the equipment, and the concentrator
spun like a top before her eyes and disappeared from her field
of vision, from her memory, and from her consciousness. Ruzhena Mirakova, intern at the Institute of Telepathy, twenty-
three years old, disappeared, too.

Only the strange, inexplicable feeling of ethereal lightness remained.

It felt as though billions of invisible strings attached to her
body were pulling in all directions, and she were getting bigger
and bigger. It was clear that something absolutely amazing was
about to happen.

Pure, marvelous rapture filled her. Ruzhena saw—though that
is not the word to describe Ruzhena's feelings—she came to
know the life of her planet in a fraction of a second. She came
to know the myriad feelings and thoughts of man, his complex
and paradoxical spirit. She felt unbelievably big, enlarged to
monstrous proportions. And at the same time, she knew that
deep inside she was the same little Ruzhena. But millions of
newborn babies were crying in her, and hundreds of thousands
of dying people were whispering in her, and crowds of people
were laughing and crying, working, resting, thinking, and playing. They were all called one thing—people—and they all lived
within her.

Feeling them inside herself, in her soul, was a once-in-a-lifetime
pleasure, and it was killing Ruzhena. Short lightning jabs of
pain pierced her body as it embraced the earth. . . .

Skinny Shchapov was angry. He snorted, shook his head, and hunched his shoulders.

"What's the problem, oh wonderful one?" the plump woman who shared his lab inquired. She looked up from her microscope and pushed her glasses up into her hair. Her tired pale-blue eyes looked into Shchapov's.

"Tata, I think I'm losing my mind."

"I think that happened a long time ago."

"Don't joke about it." He toyed with a piece of film he had just developed and held it up to the light for the hundredth time. "You know, yesterday, when I was going over to take pictures, I ran into Ruzhena Mirakova, that intern of Ermolov's, in the hall. I had my camera with me, and I offered to take her picture. The light was right: oblique, sunlight on the floor. She's a good natured girl, and she agreed. I took pictures every which way, full front, profile, against the window, in the shade, in the sun. A whole roll. And I developed it today and ... well. ..."

Shchapov handed the roll to Tata. She looked at it and turned to him in surprise.

"You took pictures of an empty hallway?"

"Looks like it!"

She shook her head.

"Listen, Shchapov, I have a friend who's a great shrink. Hallucinations, raving in broad daylight ... those are right up his alley. He can help you."

"Go see your shrink yourself!"

Ermolov changed considerably during those days. His black eyebrows took on an even more pronounced arch, trying to climb off his face and into his hair. His mad yellow eyes burned with an impatient flame.

Three large videophones took up a quarter of his office, and faces never left the screens. Ermolov would speak with several colleagues at once, some in the room, some on the phone. Ermolov rumbled and grumbled like a volcano.

Pavel, the chief custodial engineer, had been waiting a long time to see Ermolov. He was about to go see the director instead, when Ermolov got a few free minutes.

"What's the problem, Pavel?" Ermolov asked, lighting a cigarette and blowing smoke rings into the sunbeam that crossed his office.

The engineer hemmed and hawed.

"It's like this, Dr. Ermolov," he said, choosing his words carefully. "I wanted to talk to you about your intern Ruzhena Mirakova."

"What about her?"

"She's working at night."

"On what?"

"I don't know, I just know she's working at night. I was on duty last night and going down the hall. I saw a light on in 108. I rattled the doorknob. It was locked. I knocked, no one answered. Suddenly Mirakova appeared. It was so sudden that, to tell you the truth, she scared me. 'What are you doing?' I ask. 'Working,' she says. 'I have an experiment I can't leave.' 'What kind of an experiment at two in the morning?' I ask. 'That's how it is,' she says. You have to set her straight. And if she really needs to work nights, then she should get a pass from the administration."

"Hold on, Pavel," Ermolov interrupted the old man. "You're mixed up here. Room 108 isn't Mirakova's lab. That's what's-his-name's, Arefyev's. He's on vacation."

"All the more reason. And I'm telling you, that girl is strange. There's something weird about her."

The old man waved his fingers in the air, trying to make his feelings clearer.

"Just a minute," Ermolov said, turning in his chair. He reached for one of the videophones and turned it on. "Here's 108," he said. "And something is going on in there." He could see Arefyev's concentrator, filling the room with yellow light. The slight young woman was sitting with her back to the screen, her head resting on the back of the chair. He could see her pure, high forehead and her thick hair.

"Mirakova! Ruzhena!" Ermolov called. She did not stir and her hands hung lifelessly from the chair.

"Something's wrong with her," Ermolov said, turning to the old man.

Pavel got up. By then there were six people in Ermolov's office, staring in horror at the image on the screen.

"Let's go," Ermolov said, turning off the phone.

They ran down the institute's echoing corridors. They were surprised to see Ruzhena slowly heading down the shiny hallway to her lab. Ermolov called out to her, but she had gone into the room. They ran in after her.

Silence reigned in the room. There was a layer of dust on everything. Ruzhena was staring in silence at the still equipment; the dials weren't turning and the lights weren't blinking.

"Ruzhena!"

She turned. Ermolov was shocked by her pallor. She seemed to be recognizing them slowly, and a timid smile came to her lips.

"What was the matter with you just now?" Ermolov asked.

She looked at him in surprise. Pavel ran out of the room. As if responding to a common impulse, they all ran out after him. Ruzhena slowly followed.

Ermolov reached the door to room 108 and kicked it open.

Yellow light was pouring from Arefyev's concentrator. Mirakova lay back in the chair in front of the machine. Her wide-open eyes were glazed.

Ermolov grabbed her hand, but feeling the iciness of the corpse, dropped it. The hand thudded against the chair.

"She's dead," he announced, licking his dry lips.

They all turned, and expecting something even more horrible, peered down the length of the long hall. They waited.

It was empty. Just a hallway. Windows along the left side, doors along the right. White ceiling, linoleum with pink flecks on the floor. Treetops, an air-conditioning unit, and a forklift for the institute warehouse showed through the windows.

A woman's figure turned down the hallway and slowly came toward them. It was she.

When she was close and they could see that it was Ruzhena Mirakova, they gasped. Only Ermolov, after a quick second look at the body in the chair, asked her loudly:

"What is the meaning of this, Ruzhena?"

She smiled with her timid smile and moved her lips. And they realized that they did not hear her words. There was no sound. Ruzhena's thoughts penetrated their minds directly.

"I'm dead. I died three days ago."

They rushed up to the young woman. Their hands collided in the air. For a few seconds they touched and squeezed each other's hands. Finally Pavel couldn't stand it any longer. "Oh, my God," he shouted and bolted from the room. Ermolov and the others followed. They ran like boys from a nightmare come true. They slowed down to a fast walk and came to a stop in front of Ermolov's office. Not a word had been said. A group gathered around them. The young people observed their supervisors' strange behavior with interest. Ermolov took out a large checked handkerchief and wiped his brow. Others straightened their ties and collars.

"Immediately ... conference ... all staff members," sighed Ermolov and disappeared behind his door.

The crowd did not disperse. The bizarre rumor kept spreading. People conferred anxiously.

"You see, Tata," Shchapov said to the tiny blonde with the pale-blue eyes, "your psychiatrist would have done nothing for me. I never doubted the scientific objectivity of the film and I was absolutely right."

Someone suggested they go see how things were. The crowd hurried up to the third floor, where Sergei's and Ruzhena's rooms were. But Ermolov had ordered the corridor blocked off, and the sensation-seekers were left unsatisfied. They stared into the frosted glass over the door but couldn't see the slightest movement.

Meanwhile there was a stormy meeting in Ermolov's office. Ermolov had regained his usual businesslike demeanor.

"Of course, we looked ridiculous," he said, "running away from that sweet child. But we had cause for worry. Ruzhena's death hasn't been explained yet. I have a suspicion that that damned concentrator has something to do with it. It's still working, even as we speak. So actually we did the right thing to run when we did. Otherwise ... otherwise, there might have been a calamity. But we are scientists, and it is our duty to study this phenomenon. But the study must be carried out carefully, in accordance with the basic safety methods, although I can't imagine what methods would be of use in this case."

After much discussion it was decided to turn Ruzhena's body over to the medical personnel. Sergei's concentrator elicited many varied opinions. Some called for its immediate destruction. Others wanted it isolated. Coming to no firm decision, they decided to leave everything as it was and recall Sergei from his vacation. Let him figure out his own apparatus.

The institute was abuzz. People stopped work in order to discuss Ruzhena's ghost. Some had managed to get up to the third floor and see Ruzhena. They returned subdued.

Ermolov's crazy day did not end with that. Toward the end of the day he got Karabichev's letters. He slit open a foreign envelope and skimmed the page.

Karabichev wrote that he had found his wife in difficult and pathetic straits. He promised to tell him all about it when he returned. Rioli was a marvelous man. At present Karabichev was sick, lolling around in the hospital, and hoped to be out soon. He was writing the letter with one aim—to share some very important ideas with Ermolov.

"I am convinced," Karabichev wrote, "that our respected Ivan Pavlovich, who created the map of the distribution of the W-effect, is wrong. It's a matter of faulty premises. Now that I've spent time here in Bessano, I've observed a number of things that lead me to suspect a possible error in Ivan Pavlovich's calculations.

"He felt that the primary parameter characterizing mutual overlay was its strength. And he measured this strength by the distance at which two people began sensing each other. The bigger the distance, the greater the strength. At first glance it seemed right. But actually, it's just the opposite. Thus, according to Ivan Pavlovich's calculations, the W-effect is five times stronger in Bessano than in Moscow. And it's true that you begin to sense people at a distance of two or three yards here, while in Moscow it's at half a yard.

"But it's more than just distance in question here. The intensity of the sensation is important, too. In Bessano the effect arises at large distances, but it's exactly five times weaker than in Moscow. Thus, the power of the effect must be measured in terms of its intensity, not the distance of its action. This idea made me reconsider Ivan Pavlovich's map.

"My dear research director, I have come to a surprising conclusion! The source of the radiation is not located in the Pacific Ocean, near Cape Horn, as we had thought. It is eight hundred miles southeast of Moscow."

Chapter 7

SERGEI WAS DREAMING of glory, fame, recognition, and unconditional victory. He dreamed of long hours of meetings and conferences, of standing at the podium head held high, modest, confident, all-knowing. Then of long months of condescending explanations to others, and long years of respect and unshakable authority.

Sergei glanced up at Erik. His face did not reveal whether he heard fame's fanfare, which was thundering in Sergei's ears. The line between his eyebrows meant that Erik was worrying about something. Sergei grunted interrogatively. Erik looked up after a long silence.

"It's a funny thing," he said thoughtfully.

"What are you talking about?"

"Think for yourself. It's so complex and yet as simple as two plus two. Nature is mirrored in man, recorded, so to speak, in his feelings, thoughts, memories—"

"Don't mix things up. Memory and thought are properties of living things, not inorganic nature."

"All right, in the form of sensation. Nature is mirrored in man in the form of his feelings. That's the first stage. Man is mirrored in the biotosis in the form of impulses that are transmitted by some subquantal biofield. That's the second step. Perhaps, it's—"

"We'll have so many problems with the second stage that we may never even get to the third," Sergei said jokingly.

"Yes, of course, but you didn't get my meaning." Erik's eyes seemed to have melted in his pale face. "The higher the degree of reflection, the higher the independence of the reacting object. That's the trick. For example, man vis-à-vis a rock...."

Sergei stared intently at Erik.

"The biotosis would have to be capable of digesting information on its own. It would have to encode the signals, remember them, compare them," he said.

"And what makes you think that it's incapable of learning how to do that?" chided Erik. He spoke evenly and softly; he seemed dispassionate, but his friend could tell by the strange paleness of his eyes that Erik was breaking through some difficult mental barrier.

"Why would it need to?" Sergei asked after some thought.

"A question like that is meaningless. It's like asking nature why it created a rational man. The autonomy of random processes plays a role in all this."

Erik stopped. He gazed out the window. So did Sergei. The biotosis glowed out there like a lighthouse. Sergei found the light blinding, scalding, like the equatorial sun. Erik looked out the window without seeming to notice the flickering glow coming through the glass.

"I'm afraid," he said, moving about in his bed. "I'm worried what the biotosis might become vis-à-vis man."

"What?"

"What man is vis-à-vis nature."

The doctor, who had been deep in his armchair and cigarette smoke, sat up.

"Could it be possible? The biotosis was created by man, and its existence is determined by the total potential tension exerted by your hypothetical biofield, generated by mankind."

"Man was created by nature and is dependent on it," Erik rebutted softly, "but that does not stop him from actively interfering in the affairs of nature. The biotosis, if it becomes independent, may want to make some changes too."

Sergei looked pityingly at Erik. Such a clear, deep mind and such a cowardly thought.

It's time to grow wings, thought Sergei. Time to push off from the earth and soar high, watching the faces and tears of the people below melt into nothingness.

"All right," he said, getting up. "I'm off."

"Right now?" Erik asked.

"Yes, not a minute to lose."

"Can't you stay till morning?"

"No time. The biotosis is developing, and we can expect new angles any time."

"Yes, Sergei, you go and tell them all what's happening, and come back quickly. I'll stay with Erik," the doctor said.

"What about your family?"

"That's not for you to worry about. You act and don't worry about Khokai-Rokh. Everything will be fine here."

Sergei took Erik's hand.

"Listen, Sergei," Erik said, frowning, "I don't know for sure yet, but . . . but I don't like that thing out there very much." He pointed toward the window. "I don't want to rain on your parade and all. But you must be objective. We can't overestimate our success. Do you understand? So don't go overboard there, OK?"

"OK, OK. Relax, old buddy." Sergei squeezed Erik's hand.

He quickly loaded the files, film, slides, and tapes into the trunk, got into the aerocar, and flew out into the mists. The sky and the earth were almost the same black color.

The car soared over the earth at an altitude of thirty yards. Sergei kept looking at the dials on the illuminated dashboard impatiently.

First thing is to make a sensational report, he thought. Open people's eyes. It'll be a bombshell! The whole learned council and some invited specialists. Then apply for a dozen patents for the biotosis in our names.

But first I think we should apply for a discoverer's patent. It's a discovery, after all! Then a few long articles in the central papers, a couple of interviews and.... Everything will be fine, it'll be terrific. Finally, a real, honest-to-goodness discovery! It's no groundless research into the influence of endless influences—this is real! Great! Important! Something worth living for, dreaming about, making mistakes for. It's finally gold! No more hanging around the sidelines of science. Hold on, you crawling empiricists, here I come.

Sergei reached Moscow four hours later. Even though it was early morning, the aerocars were three deep on the main roads, and Sergei had a lot of trouble getting to his turnoff. He parked in the yard, lowering the heavy vehicle onto the damp asphalt, and ran up to his apartment.

His father was out. The apartment still smelled of tobacco and the warm night air. The windows were shut and the ventilation was off.

Sergei opened the windows and then took a shower. The large cold drops drummed on his hairy chest. His dusky skin grew taut. Sergei rotated in the shower, spitting up little fountains of crystal water. Ten minutes later he sat in a chair, relaxed, and listened to currents of white lightning coursing through his body.

The city had awakened and was working at full throttle, an engine with millions upon millions of people-power. It might never have been asleep at all. Sergei listened to the clatter of life coming in the window and thought about how he, a tiny person, a ten-millionth part of the energetic mass that lived and worked in Moscow, would be famous and known to all of them in an hour's time. Everybody who walked, thought, and reasoned would know him. He pictured billions of people in different places and at different times dropping what they were doing for a minute—the assembly line, the desk, the field, the lab, the car, the tennis court—wherever they were. Just to hear his name.

Short and long radio waves, pulsating, would transmit the signals for the news report with his name and Erik's. The signal would race around the globe, eliciting a sigh of relief and awe from the world. This city would give birth to a new power, a new strength. And it would be done by him, a tiny man, a ten-millionth particle, a cell of the city, an unrecognized scientist. . . .

Suddenly a daring thought came to him. What if he didn't go anywhere or tell anyone? Would life's complex mechanism get started then?

Sergei thought and decided that it would. The secret of the biotosis would be revealed. If not he, then Erik; if not Erik, then someone else would tell. In the final analysis people always solved the tasks they set for themselves.

Why do dreams come true? Because a dream is the first plan for work in the direction that interests a man. And if people make up a plan, they follow it . . . if not today, then tomorrow.

He heard a scream. Someone was calling for help. Sergei clutched the arms of the chair, but didn't get up. He listened closely. The screams died down for a minute. Then he could hear the sobbing, pleading voice again. A woman was crying and moaning somewhere.

Sergei grabbed his pants and ran for the door. He pushed the lock button with one hand and tried to pull on his pants with the other. The door flew open and the pants fell on the floor. Sergei tossed them aside and ran out onto the landing. There was no one there; the noise was coming from the fourth floor. Sergei went back in, put on his pants and jacket, and ran up-stairs two steps at a time.

There was a woman panting in the open door of apartment 405. Her shoulders and bosom heaved with sobs. Her gray hair, once set in an ornate hairdo, fell limply to her shoulders. An old man and a girl looked on anxiously. The girl was giving the woman a drink, and the woman's teeth chattered against the glass. The water dribbled down her chin, gathering into small shimmering drops.

"What happened?"

The old man, who was muttering something soothing in the woman's ear, looked up at Sergei. The newspaper in his hand was rolled up, giving the famous movie star on the page a long and surprised-looking face.

"Her husband died," he explained.

"Of what?"

"Of death," the old man said angrily and turned his back on him. Sergei wanted to come closer, but was afraid of the W-effect. He did not want to wallow in the marshy waves of human misery.

"It's the times, my dear," the old man said vaguely. "Don't take it to heart, darling."

"Should we call the police?" the girl with the glass asked, carefully peering into the apartment.

"I woke up last night and saw him sitting on my bed." The woman started crying again.

"I'll go look," the girl said firmly, and squeezing between the woman and the doorway, went in the entry.

"Be careful there!" the old man called after her.

"Where's her husband?" Sergei asked softly.

"I told you he's dead. Buried yesterday."

Sergei felt his head spinning.

"Then who's she talking about?"

"About him, the husband! Boy, you're slow! You haven't been home long, have you?"

"No, I haven't."

The girl shot out of the apartment. She was waving the empty glass wildly.

"It's a nightmare!" she shouted and ran down the stairs. "A corpse!"

"What corpse?"

The woman looked at him suspiciously. "Haven't you heard?" she asked carefully.

"He's behind the times, he hasn't heard a thing."

"It happens nowadays. Not with everybody, but it does happen. My husband died, I buried him, went to see my sister in Kashir, came home, and found him in the spot where he had fallen down dead. You can imagine my reaction! I thought I was going mad, I was so scared. He was gone and yet he was right there, underfoot."

Sergei stared at the woman.

"That has to be . . . examined," he muttered.

"What's to examine? Life is cracking up all over the planet," the old man said philosophically.

"I don't know how I'm going to live now," the woman said bitterly. "I'm afraid to go into my room."

Sergei shuddered, picturing the horror of the situation. He bent his head and quickly left.

That day Ermolov felt the full brunt of Sergei's temper. Sergei demanded a convocation of the Greater Learned Council plus all the commissions of the Academy of Sciences, plus all the committees dealing with the mutual overlay.

"I have to have some realistic guarantee that your announcement is of great scientific interest," Ermolov said coldly, watching Sergei.

He seemed an entirely different person. What had happened to the melancholy self-control, the calm, the restraint that hid his mockery of his colleagues? Sergei was ready to go into battle. Why? What had happened?

"My only guarantee is my conscience as a scientist. What I am about to reveal should belong to humanity."

"Why? Why couldn't we hear what you have to say in a more intimate group first?"

"Intimate groups are for telling jokes," Sergei said rudely. "And I'll be talking about things that our entire country, the whole world, should know."

Ermolov thought a bit.

"All right," he said. "Here's the situation. Today there's an enlarged meeting of the United Council, to discuss ways of combatting the telepathic phenomena on our planet. There will be many important people there. Academicians, and members of our Learned Council. As an exception, I will let you speak. But keep it short. We'll leave in twenty minutes."

The meeting hall for the United Council was a large, dull room with a vast number of tables, chairs, and chandeliers. Sergei sat by the wall, the loaded projector and tape recorder at his feet, the folder with his report on his lap. He looked around excitedly. Lots of bald pates and gold-rimmed glasses. Unhurried movements. People full of self-confidence. Solid. Firm.

I'll shake you guys up, Sergei thought triumphantly. He was

not afraid, but his fingers toyed with the folder and his heart beat rapidly.

After several long minutes of the day's announcements the floor was given to Ivan Pavlovich, professor of telepathy. The old man went onstage and unrolled the by-now-familiar map, showing the areas of varying intensity of the W-effect.

Ivan Pavlovich told them about Karabichev's idea. The professor did not rush; he rounded off his phrases, and Sergei could feel his bile rising.

"Thus, if we measure the strength of the mutual overlay effect not in terms of distance but in the power of its action, then the maximum will fall not into the Pacific Ocean, as we had earlier supposed, but in this very spot here."

The professor's pointer slid southeast from Moscow along the map to a small circle.

"We are exploring that area right now. I do not know if we will find anything, but we must test Karabichev's hypothesis."

Sergei stood. His voice, hoarse and breaking, sounded unexpectedly loud.

"I can answer that question."

The members of the council began whispering. Sergei approached the dais and stood next to Ivan Pavlovich.

"This is our next speaker," the chairman explained.

"Please, Comrade . . . eh . . . Arefyev."

"I shall try to be brief, but my subject is a broad one. If I begin to bore you, let me know, and I'll start condensing. All right," he said as he got closer to the podium and checked how they were setting up the projector, "I'll do this chronologically, so as not to get confused.

"Humanity has witnessed the discovery of an elemental force. These things happen in our times, when inventors have very narrow fields of specialization and cannot grasp their subject in all its many facets.

"Two years ago Erik Erdman obtained a mutant from a seaweed that was capable of synthesizing linear polymers from the air's oxygen and carbon dioxide. You see the flower on the slide. It is called a biotosis. That is the mutant.

"Further work was done by both of us—Erdman and me. We wanted to make the biotosis industrially viable, but things weren't working out. The biotosis was obviously limited in its possibilities. We were unable to obtain good results. The topic was basically closed and we worked at it half-heartedly. But we had a stroke of luck. It happens in science. But rarely. We accidentally discovered the optimal conditions for the biotosis' growth.

"Comrades, I see questions and puzzlement on your faces. You have every right to ask, What do polymers and this biotosis have to do with us? I understand. You will soon see the connection between the mutual overlay effect and what I am talking about. Be patient.

"Thus, we have established that the biotosis grew in stuffy, warm places filled with . . . people. Why people? What did people have to do with it? We could not answer those questions then. Now we know the correct answer.

"But six months ago we were only interested in how to grow the biotosis in quantities sufficient for analyses, tests, and industrial synthesis. Having discovered its ability to grow in direct contact with masses of people, we began using it. We placed tanks with the biotosis in movie houses, clubs, and meeting halls. The biotosis would get a push and then go on developing independently. Its further growth, it seemed to us, did not depend on the presence of human beings. This was confirmed by our experiments.

"Having gathered several pounds of the biotosis, we went out to the Khokai-Rokh Biostation. And a miracle happened. By placing several pieces of the biotosis into a common mass, we created what amounted to an atomic explosion in its development. In a few hours the weight of the biomass reached over one hundred million tons. Here is the slide. You see that even now the biotosis is still shaped like a flower with a baroque configuration. It filled a huge quarry and grew another hundred yards above it. This happened the night of August fifteenth of this year. I ask you to take note of the date, as I'm sure it's a familiar one to you. Then the sharp increase in its size and weight ceased. It is still growing in volume, but very slowly.

"At the present time, a mountain of this biopolymer rises above the steppe near the Khokai-Rokh Biostation. From a distance, it looked like a large steppe burial mound. By the way,

Khokai-Rokh is located seven hundred and fifty miles from Moscow and is right in the center of that circle drawn on Ivan Pavlovich's map based on Karabichev's theories.

"I can see from your excitement that you have grasped the thought I am trying to convey. Precisely! The biotosis in its present state is the mysterious, long-sought source of the radiation that is harassing all of mankind.

"I won't dwell in detail on how we reached this conclusion. I will only say that we were aided by nighttime photography of the biotosis. You see, the biotosis glows. In these slides you see the total light coming from the flower. It's a beautiful sight at night. But if you look closely—it's best to view this with a magnifier—you will see billions of glowing dots under the surface. These dots are in constant motion and interaction. We undertook a statistical determination of the biotosis' light—in short, counting the number of glowing dots in separate parts—and came to an unanticipated discovery of this polymer's marvelous properties. I won't describe the process of our ideas and experiments. I will only give you the conclusions.

"First, the polymer we call the biotosis is capable of absorbing all kinds of emanations produced by the brain and the human nervous system and recording them in the form of specific, glowing molecular associations."

Sergei leaned down and turned on the tape recorder.

"You will hear Erdman's thoughts on the matter."

After a moment of tape hiss, Erik's voice said:

"People have been positing the existence of a single biofield on earth for a long time. Today the direct and oblique facts of the distribution of telepathic signals are the object of serious scientific research. The nature of this phenomenon has not been clear until now. Work on the biotosis has led us to some information on the matter. We theorize that the biofield has a subquantal character. This means that the transmission of the signals is accompanied by subquantal transfers of some particles and holes from one energy level to another. This breaking up of the level gives rise to an emanation that has yet to be observed by any transponders invented by man. Only the human organism, and the brain in particular, is capable of reacting to these waves. The motion of the signal in the biotosis, or, as it's also called, the psi-phenomenon, has many special properties. The signal is dispersed almost immediately, it does not depend on the medium, and it does not weaken with distance, and may even grow stronger. In general, I feel that the emanation may be dissipated at great distance from the source. We have determined that a minuscule amount of energy is needed to create a telepathic signal. This is understandable, since a subquantal exchange represents only one ten-thousandth of a usual exchange of an electron from one orbit to another, and secondly, any movement of a signal in a biofield becomes increased through the resonance of the oscillations. It is also clear that such an increase would be uneven and fluctuating."

Sergei turned off the tape recorder. No one spoke.

"The resolution. Point one: I want to reiterate that the biotosis can register all the psi-signals given off by humanity with the speed of light. Now I move to point two.

"It can be formulated in the following manner. The biotosis itself is a source of emanations of the second order. It receives a signal and feeds it back to the source in either weakened or strengthened form. The process is similar to the reflection of waves from an obstacle. However, such an analogy is too crude. The biotosis is capable of processing information. The signal it receives is not reflected immediately, nor in the same direction. We call this property the uncontrolled feedback, although we now suspect that this is an incorrect characterization. In other words, everything that happens in the biotosis is reflected in people. It's as though it tugs at the molecules that form people's nerves with invisible subquantal threads.

"Point three."

Sergei took a breath. He felt the eyes of the audience on him. He lost his train of thought and stopped. The hall waited.

"The rest of the points," he finally said, "are deductions from the first two. There is a polymer, called the biotosis, which is capable of perceiving, registering, and sending out, again in accordance with its own laws, all the signals that occur on the subquantal biofield of the earth. Since people are the transponders of these signals, they have all become connected to the biotosis since its inception. Every person and all of humanity are 'recorded' on the biotosis in its various parts in the form of associations of agitated molecules. The geometric movement of a person from one place to another is accompanied by a movement in the associations on the biotosis."

"Does the signal travel on the biotosis the way people travel on earth?" someone asked loudly from the back.

"Yes . . . I mean, no." Sergei smiled, collected his thoughts, and went on. "Let's not liken the biotosis to the earth. The movement of an object and the distribution of the impulse on the biotosis cannot be equivalent. But they are connected somehow."

The din in the room grew.

"The instantaneous creation of hundreds of tons of a biotosis is against the laws of thermodynamics," came a shout.

"Clarify, please," Sergei asked.

The person who had called out got up, blushed, blanched, and then spoke, stuttering.

"The instantaneous formation of hundreds of millions of tons of biotosis from inorganic material rather than monomers, which contain the necessary energy reserves, should have catastrophic results."

"The biotosis is a seaweed mutant," Sergei responded. "A mutant that multiplies quickly, the way microbes do, increasing their mass by thousands of times in a twenty-four-hour period. Let's not confuse the vital activity of the biotosis with inorganic synthesis, all right?"

The young man wanted to argue, but there was a call from the audience to continue.

"Questions later! Let him talk! Let him talk!"

"With your permission, comrades, I'll continue. So, the biotosis simultaneously perceives all the sensory, psychological, and intellectual information of humanity, stores it, and sorts it. Five large zones are apparent on the biotosis, which correspond to man's five senses. But it also has close to a hundred other zones whose meaning is not yet clear to us. Erdman theorizes that these are areas of man's subconscious and of humanity's untapped resources. Comrades! The biotosis is the brain and the soul of humanity. It registers all of the many facets of man's life at once. Newborn infants cry, dying people say goodbye, lovers meet, travelers depart, billions of people work, rest, sleep, and amuse themselves in it. And all of it is registered with the constant motion of the lights under its cold surface. Every man has been given his double, who lives in the World Soul. Every change in a man is immediately felt by his double in the biotosis, and conversely, the double's behavior takes its toll on the man in some very strange ways.

"How can we explain all these strange things that don't let mankind rest, bringing both joy and sorrow? Very simply.

"When people come close to one another, their doubles in the biotosis are brought together as well. At a certain distance the molecular groupings in the biotosis begin to exchange energy and unite into a common structural unit, forming a complicated vacillating complex. The real people sense this immediately. It seems to them that the neighbor with whom they are in contact has climbed into their souls, their brains, their bodies. This is the essence of the W effect. It is explained by the simple short circuiting of the molecular associations in the World Soul.

"Comrades! We observed completely inexplicable events on the fifteenth of August. Now their cause is clear. When we joined the pieces of the biotosis, thereby creating the critical mass necessary for the chain-reaction growth, the emanations of all the people living on the earth cascaded down on the biotosis like a waterfall. The molecular agitation spread chaotically throughout the biotosis. This was accompanied by collisions of associations. The energy of their interaction was so great, and the emanation so strong, that in individual cases the living objects changed the characteristic pattern of their nervous system.

"The biotosis has a unique characteristic. The received emanation and the doubles' emanations depend on distance. The farther away a person is from the Khokai-Rokh Biostation, the more blurred the association and the weaker the feedback. This means that as a function of distance the World Soul's influence on people lessens, even though the radius of its effect increases. As you see, the mistake of the first hypothesis has finally been explained.

"A few words on pseudoresurrection. A person dies, but a record of his intellectual and emotional history remains in the World Soul. But since the energy flow ceases with death, the record stays immobile—that is, dark. But if a living person nears the place of death, his double in the biotosis stimulates the molecular 'soul' of the deceased, and it begins to emit its usual characteristic code waves. The deceased is resurrected. But he 'lives' only in the consciousness of the people near him. And with time the 'molecular soul' should fade, because the chaotic action of its neighbors will destroy the association's structure. You could say that it's fatal for the deceased to associate with the living.

"Comrades! I can see your impatience. You must have a thousand questions. In answering them, I will be able to explain the rest of the World Soul's properties. In conclusion, as one of the inventors of the World Soul, I would like to say that our epoch has been given a great acquisition. And we must safeguard it."

Sergei stopped. The room was silent.

Finally someone called out: "What proof, actual proof, do you have for what you say?"

Sergei smiled and shrugged.

"I can show you film," he said, "or give you our test results, calculations, and observations. If that won't suffice, let's go to Khokai-Rokh and watch it together."

"Wait," Ermolov interrupted. "How much autonomy does the World Soul have? I mean, what can we expect from it?"

"I don't know," Sergei announced firmly.

"Anything you like," came a sarcastic remark.

"Quiet! Let him talk."

"Comrades, please don't demand the impossible from me. I've told you everything we've been able to find out through our painstaking work in Khokai-Rokh. What I will say now will represent my own theories. They may materialize, but they may turn out to be radically wrong. We feel that the biotosis is developing. I think that as compared to people, it has different ways of processing information. I think it's beginning to develop elements of consciousness. For instance, just recently I tried to cut off a piece of the biotosis for analysis—"

"Taking a knife to the World Soul! These scientists hold nothing sacred," said a little old scientist, coughing ironically.

"I could not get a sample, because the biotosis did not want me to. The World Soul resisted violently."

A whisper traveled across the room. The scientists were shaking their heads.

"I have a question." The speaker, with a deep, strong voice, looked at Sergei calmly and seriously with his small gray eyes. "What do you think? Is your polymer a danger to society, to the lives of individuals, to the society we are building? Well, not now, perhaps, but in a few years, say? You just said yourself that it's developing and progressing."

Sergei thought about it.

"The World Soul on its own is helpless. Its strength lies in its ability to influence individuals and humanity as a whole. The moral quality of the biotosis is determined by the people who are 'recorded' on it. I don't think that any antagonism will arise, but you can't foresee everything. I believe in the World Soul's best qualities. Up until now it's only brought good."

"Well, that depends on your definitions."

Sergei was incensed.

"You should be ashamed of yourselves, comrades! The World Soul has united millions of people, and distrust and deception have disappeared. Life is simpler and happier. Isn't that all for the good?"

A powerful roar drowned out his voice. They weren't listening to each other, those calm, majestic men. They were expressing their reactions frankly and emotionally. They banged on the tables, gestured, laughed. Ermolov brought order to the room.

"We must study everything in great detail," he said, "and then we will think about what to do with the World Soul. If it is as Arefyev says, an All-World Congress will have to be convened and the decision will be out of our hands."

People were calming down. The members of the council took turns speaking on Sergei's report.

Sergei did not listen. He had turned himself off. He felt that he had worked long and hard, and he was tired. He sat there resting. They didn't understand. They didn't appreciate it, he thought sadly.

He got home late and exhausted. The tension was gone and there was only fatigue. If only Erik were here. Why were they so hostile to me? he thought. Or did I just imagine it? It was all so different from what I had imagined—so stupid! Sergei felt a hand on his shoulder. It was his father. His face was pale and tired.

"I heard you . . . and your temperamental display," he said. "Well, you sure came up with a tricky thing. Congratulations. But what do you really think about it?" He waved his hand in the air vaguely. "Are you happy with it?"

Sergei jumped up.

"Very much. It's what people have been dreaming about. Unity, mutual understanding, communication without lies or cheating. Absolute trust, no barriers between people."

His father lunged into a chair and watched his son thoughtfully.

"This is the materialization of our wildest dreams!" Sergei went on. "Is marriage without love, without total mutual sharing of human feelings, without complete mutual understanding now possible? Impossible. Is the moral loneliness that every person is doomed to physically now possible? No, because now he will find not only words from his neighbors, but sincere feelings that he can live by just as he lives by his own. People will become immeasurably richer; the scope of their feelings has grown from the single 'I' to the four billion 'we.' It's the end of endless depression, the end of 'everyone dies alone.' People have become brothers physically, materially."

Sergei stopped short. He was very excited. His father was looking at him as though seeing him for the first time.

"Calm down," he said quietly. "You should talk about things like that with a clear mind."

Sergei smirked. His father walked across the room.

"Your biotosis, or World Soul, as you call it," he said, "which I cannot accept, since the soul of the world can only be the community of people working on the solution to a great and significant problem, is, simply speaking, a biological automaton of complex construction. This automaton perceives all of mankind's knowledge, feelings, and thoughts and somehow processes them. It has material and logical autonomy that permits it to control through its emanations the activity of individuals and entire societies. Now people have suddenly been given a controller that interferes in their private lives and individual plans, controls their emotions and feelings. And on top of that it turns out that your World Soul is subject to its own development. It evolves quickly. Very quickly. Understand me, I already agree with those who consider the biotosis an invention of genius. It is one of contemporary science's greatest achievements. But it's elemental. Uncontrollable. That's the danger in it. Atomic energy was also a great achievement for its time. But it could bring death, horrible death. And it too was an elemental, uncontrollable force.

"Our society is distinguished by the fact that we build it consciously. We control our future. We create it with our own hands, and we don't need an automaton correcting our work, however smart and wise it may be."

"But why not?" Sergei exclaimed. "The World Soul unites and universalizes the experiences of four billion people! It contains all the great moral principles. Do you think it's stupider or worse than any individual person? Why do you think. . . ."

He stopped.

"Finish," his father said. "I understood your thought. A man must be in control. Only a man, and not a supercybernetic machine or your biotosis. For only a man can understand his people, and its needs and hopes. The government changes, but the people stay. And it will always be people who will be in power, people with warm human feelings, with red blood, with faith in their hearts, and with all their faults and virtues."

They both were silent.

"Your invention should be used," his father continued. "It has much that is useful and necessary to offer humanity. But as long as it is a thing unto itself, it is dangerous. It is not for nothing that our all efforts and the efforts of our ancestors and children are to make the future controllable. It is unknowable. It is very difficult to see anything accurately through the dark curtains of time. You should give your life to ensure that it will be the way the heroes of the past envisioned it. And instead you open a box with a devil in it, and the devil gets on your back! In a sense you are criminals. You are excused only by the unpredictability that is inherent in any kind of scientific endeavor.

But you have created a monster. And now you must discover the antidote. It's possible that you will have to destroy your World Soul and start creating something else."

"No!" shouted Sergei. "Never!"

His father grasped his hands.

"You were just talking with enthusiasm about the marvelous action of the mutual overlay effect on people, on human society. But Ermolov in his introduction said just the contrary. Tens of thousands of families have been broken by the W-effect. People who used to love and respect each other can't stand to be near each other now. Ermolov maintains that since contact between people is taking an analogous path, the possibility of conscious control of one's actions is disappearing. People have lost confidence in themselves, in their actions and reactions. There is too much of the unpredictable in life. This all takes its toll on the productivity of labor and the general discipline and moral atmosphere of our society. Just take these pseudoresurrections! Unbelievable chaos. What do we need with these ghosts?"

"Why are all of you harping on the ghosts?" Sergei screamed. "What are you afraid of? They don't threaten anyone, and anyway they'll de-evolve with time and disappear!"

"The moral atmosphere of our society does not permit—"

He was interrupted by the click of the videophone in the hall. Sergei went to pick it up and saw Ermolov's face on the screen.

"Get over to the institute immediately," the scientific director said. His eyes were severe and distant.

Sergei ran out of Ermolov's office without hearing all of his explanation. He raced to the third floor.

Sergei ran up the stairs and, pushing aside the guard, threw open the door to room 108. He caught a moment when the room was completely empty. It was the briefest second, but it seemed endless. The concentrator wasn't working. The main crystal had been removed. The tables were covered with thick gray dust. A piece of paper was sticking out from a crack in the cabinet and rustling in the gust of air that had rushed in with Sergei.

And then he saw Ruzhena. She smiled quietly when she saw

him. She looked as though she had just turned off her equipment and was ready to go home.

She ran her hands over her head. Her hair cascaded onto her shoulders. It was dim in the room; the diffused evening light barely illuminated the objects in the room. But Ruzhena was sparkling in sunlight. Another paradox, Sergei thought. It seems that time is not synchronized in the World Soul with the images.

He sat for a long time, his hands around his knees. Then he looked up with swollen eyes. Ermolov, tuning in on the video-phone, saw an empty room with Sergei showing dark in the center of the room.

"I want to hold you," the young man said hoarsely. The room was silent.

"I want to hold you," Sergei repeated.

Ermolov sighed and turned off the screen.

When Ermolov tuned in again, there was no one in room 108.

Shocked and blinded, Sergei wandered around the streets of Moscow.

Sergei noticed nothing around him. He was walking mechanically down the empty sidewalks of Moscow.

Chapter 8

THE DAY WAS PEARLY. The sun broke through the haze and played on the desultory fountains. The flame-red cannas looked dull and the neatly trimmed lawns were bleak. Only in the thick shade of the plane trees did the grass look succulent and fresh. A ghostly blue-gray city was frozen in the glass walls of the large, old-fashioned building.

Erik sat on the white garden bench and, squinting in the oppressive diffuse light, absently scratched patterns in the sand with a stick. Along with the other experts of the special UN commission gathered at the congress in Moscow, Erik was to stand in judgment over the World Soul.

The documentation on the biotosis had already filled two entire rooms. The archive shelves groaned under the weight of endless file folders. Every half-hour, robot mailmen delivered sacks full of letters, packages, and telegrams. The computer center barely managed to keep up with the flood of data. They worked day and night trying to come up with an algorithm for the common consensus.

On the one hand we have cold, calm, dispassionate machines, thought Erik, and on the other, hot, prejudiced, excited people! He remembered the effect on the commission made by the report of the biomorphologist Bratsman. The Swede had appeared on the very first day of the sessions. His calm, quiet speech was weighty and convincing. He used the epitron to illustrate his point with graphs, diagrams, and all kinds of tables and charts.

"We know," he said, "that the carbon level in living organisms varies between 0.1 to 26 percent of live weight. Thus, duckweed contains 2.5 percent carbon; the bluebell, 10.2; reindeer moss, 21.8; a freshwater snail, 1.70; a crayfish, 7.49; a bee, 12.30; a mouse, 10.77; a cat, 20.56; and so on. The carbon content can vary significantly within a species depending on gender, development, and other factors. Thus the larva of the cabbage moth is 7.79 percent carbon, the pupa is 9.41, and the adult form is 19.40. The main source of carbon for plants is the carbon dioxide in the air. Animals get their carbon from food proteins, fats, and carbohydrates.

"Let us turn to the biotosis. Today its live weight is over a hundred million tons. Where did it get the carbon necessary for the creation of a biopolymer of that weight? Unfortunately, we do not know what part carbon plays in the makeup of the biotosis. But if the carbon level of *Opalinariaos medium*, which we know is approximately 10 percent, has not changed during the mutation, then we are faced with a monstrous figure: ten million tons of carbon taken from the atmosphere by the biotosis. In terms of carbon dioxide, that makes more than forty million tons of the gas.

"Let us examine the repercussions.

"First of all the climate will change. As you know, carbon dioxide retains infrared radiation, thus creating a warming effect. A depleted atmosphere will lead to lowering the average annual temperature of the earth. Plants will have to go on hunger rations, which will inevitably affect the crops. In short, the biotosis is destroying the earth's carbon-dioxide balance and can bring on serious consequences."

After the Swede's speech, many commission members called for the immediate destruction of the biotosis.

Erik knew that they had come here with their minds made up and that the Swede had only strengthened their convictions. Even Erik was disturbed by the Swede's cut-and-dried logic, even though he realized he had exaggerated the situation.

Polyanitsyn, a Soviet climatologist, read his report.

"Mr. Chairman, respected members of the commission, comrades and gentlemen," Polyanitsyn began, "I would like to add to the interesting report given by our Swedish colleague. As far as I know, there are twenty-three hundred billion tons of carbon dioxide in the atmosphere. And therefore the amount of carbon dioxide removed from the atmosphere by the biotosis will hardly constitute one thousandth of one percent of its original stores. This minuscule loss can in no way affect the carbon-dioxide balance; it is too small even to be measured. And this should reassure Mr. Bratsman. But with your permission, I would like to continue his train of thought.

"At the present time, fuel consumption alone accounts for six billion tons of carbon being thrown into the atmosphere. That is more than enough to create another hundred and fifty World Souls. Agriculture adds another two billion tons. There's another fifty biotoses for you. It only takes one eruption of a volcano like Kotopahi to replace the carbon dioxide removed from the atmosphere by the biotosis. The World Soul will not cause any climactic, thermodynamic, physical-chemical, or biological traumas. The question of its existence is primarily a moral one. So let us approach it as a human question, an ethical one, without getting sidetracked. Thank you for your attention."

"The complex of problems with which the so-called World Soul has presented us," said the Polish sociologist Danyczewski, "approaches biological collectivism. You can't dismiss this idea out of hand. Only when we have unearthed the source of development, the dialectical unity of the positive and negative aspects, can we accept or reject the idea and thereby decide the fate of the World Soul. The rising feeling of collectivism in human society, on the one hand, creates the desire for complete mutual understanding and, on the other, gives rise to its inevitable opposite: the desire to maintain one's individuality. We observe these same tendencies in the relations between human society and the World Soul. I would not be wrong if I said that ninety percent of the demand to destroy the biotosis is elicited by its psychological effects. But that is only one side of the problem, after all! The biotosis has revealed the other side too, showing us new paths of communication, demonstrating new aspects of man's creative unity.

"Recently in Warsaw three patent applications were made for a new type of protection against meteorites for interplanetary vehicles. All three designs are exactly alike down to the smallest detail. A check revealed that the inventors did not have an inkling of one another's existence. This is not a random occurrence. The biofield created by three brains working in the same direction, reflected and refracted in the spontaneous emanations of the biotosis, bound the inventors for a moment. I'm not sure that any one of them alone could have solved the problem. And what heights are being reached in medical diagnosis! We owe that to the World Soul as well. Actually, we are indebted to the physicians who are willing selflessly to submerge themselves into their patients' sensory worlds. The World Soul has brought synthetic art to life. And so we are indebted to it for the pleasure we receive from the contemporary work of poets and musicians, musicians and artists, and artists and scientists.

"As you see, the problem is not that simple. Of course, we can destroy the biotosis. But we will never be able to forget that it existed. No artificially induced amnesia or hushing up will help. Humanity will return to the biotosis sooner or later—of course, on a different level of research than now, but it will return. Wouldn't it be wiser therefore to drop completely the fatal question: to be or not to be? Let's try to protect ourselves from the harmful effects of the biotosis, but let's keep everything valuable that it has brought us." There was general applause.

"The World Soul is a sign from God," said Brother Cariolli, a representative of the Pope. "People guided by divine providence have brought us a miracle. The World Soul calls those who have strayed from the flock back into the bosom of the Roman Catholic Church. The churches are filled with worshippers. Those who raise the sword in sinful pride against the Lord's flower are being led by Satan. It is not for man to crush the World Soul. The Lord has warned the insolent by depriving them of memory and reason. And this will befall anyone who infringes on God's plan. Even in sinful Babylon—" The chairman called on Brother Cariolli to confine his remarks to the subject at hand.

"I am not religious," Professor Ortega, of the law department of Salamanca University, began his speech, "but I would like an explanation for the many strange events that have taken place recently. These events turn our conceptions of causality upside down. I won't speak without substantiation. I will read you a police report.

" 'On April seventeenth of this year at nine-thirty A.M., Señor Carada, the director of Savings and Loan Association number 16 for the Lopez Financial House, came to the police and reported that he had awakened the night before with a strange sense of anxiety. He dressed and went into the hall, where he saw a beam of light coming from under the door of the room that contained the safe. Carada was about to return to his room for the pistol that he kept under his pillow when the door opened. Carada, squeezing himself into a dark corner, saw a tall man with a mustache and a deep scar on his forehead. The man had a flashlight in one hand and was stuffing money into his coat with the other. After the thief had walked past him, Carada ran back to his room and got the gun. He returned to the hall quickly. It was empty. The door to the room was locked. Carada unlocked it and rushed over to the safe. He dialed the combination, known only to him, opened the safe, and discovered to his great surprise that the money was all there.

" 'While Señor Carada agreed that it might have been a hallucination, he begged the police to keep the safe under surveillance that night. Carada based his request on the fact that there was a large amount of money in the safe at that time which had to be safeguarded until it was deposited in the bank. Two policemen were dispatched to Señor Carada's house. That very night they apprehended a man in an attempted burglary. The tall middle-aged man was dark; eyes, yellow-green; nose, straight; distinguishing features, a deep scar on forehead. The suspect was a certain José Capasco, with a record for heroin dealing. When asked if he had been to Carada's house the night before, Capasco answered in the negative and provided an iron-clad alibi. When asked if he had ever been in that house, Capasco replied affirmatively. The suspect was carrying a flashlight, safe-cracking instruments, and a switchblade.'

"I could cite a number of similar cases of the violation of cause and effect. Obviously, the World Soul reads criminal thoughts and warns the appropriate party of danger."

"Nonsense!" Lionel Zoto, doctor of physics, smacked the table with his hand. "José Capasco had planned the crime carefully. The telepatheme reflected by the biotosis reached the brain of the appropriate person quite by accident. Hundreds of people, I'm certain of that, dreamed on the night of the sixteenth that some bum was stuffing money into his coat, but only Señor Carada was awakened by the dream and forced to look out into the hall, dripping with cold sweat. The biotosis reveals the hidden and forces people to maintain a respectful distance between themselves. There's no reason to attribute godlike traits to physical-chemical processes and to worship a random fluctuation in the subquantal field. The biotosis predicts the future! What nonsense! The biotosis only predicts what people have revealed to it, either consciously or subconsciously. I know that there is much talk about the biotosis' forecasts. That they allegedly were projected to specially gifted people. I would call them psychopaths, not psychics. I don't believe in these predictions. But even if they did happen, the way the biotosis construes the future through some extrasensory process is nothing more than an incorrect extrapolation of the present. The World Soul has no soul. Like a computer, it does not think. Its activity wreaks havoc with the psyches of certain individuals and hinders society's normal life. That is why it is necessary to destroy this insidious World Soul once and for all. And I assure you, ladies and gentlemen, that we will lose nothing by doing so. Absolutely nothing! There will be fewer hysterics in the world, that's all." There was laughter and applause.

Erik could not shake the feeling that despite all the heated argument, the biotosis' fate was sealed. The prosecutor demands the most extreme punishment, the defense counsel demands an acquittal, and the judges lean to this side and that. But everyone knows that the accused will be convicted.

"Ladies and gentlemen," said the aging English philosopher Harold Webst. "With your permission, I will tell you a story I heard from a friend.

"The day of the first nuclear test my friend awoke at one and stayed with Dr. Oppenheimer until about five. Of course, Dr. Oppenheimer was tense, even though his mind worked with its usual exceptional clarity. My friend tried to keep the assistants' anxieties over the meteorologic conditions from him. By three-thirty they had decided that perhaps they could set it off at five-thirty. The rain stopped at four, but the sky was covered with a heavy cloud cover. With time passing, their decision became firmer.

"Two minutes before the appointed time they all lay face down, feet toward the blast.

"The radio was counting down, for another group that was observing the blast. The tension was growing quickly as the moment approached and the minutes turned to seconds. Everyone in the room knew about the terrible hidden potential of the blast. The scientists felt that their calculations were correct and that the bomb had to go off, but each was suffering from some small doubt.

"Oppenheimer barely breathed. He held onto a post for ballance. The last few seconds he stared ahead and then, when the announcer shouted 'Now!' and there was a colossal burst of light, followed by the low rumble of the blast, the tension on his face was replaced by a look of great relief. Several of the observers, standing behind a shelter, were knocked off their feet by the shock waves.

"The tension in the room dissipated and people began congratulating each other. Everyone felt: This is it!

"The feeling that reigned in the shelter was that everyone connected with the birth of this new force would devote his life to make sure that it would always be used for good and never for evil."

The wizened old lord thrust his chin into the air, showing the veins on his wrinkled neck. He resembled an ancient and wise reptile. He looked around the room in silence.

"And no more than a year later this immeasurable force was unleashed for evil!

"Can a flywheel gone berserk be stopped?" the old philosopher asked softly. "History is a flywheel, it is a spiraling galaxy with sharp twists. The biotosis came into our lives by the will of chance. But chance is a manifestation of necessity. In destroying the biotosis we will be no more rid of it than we are of hydrogen bombs now that we have stopped testing them. Things that come into the world do not leave it until they have used themselves up completely. And the biotosis is fated to live through its own tortuous evolution.

"I just told you of a fateful moment in human history, with humanity standing on the brink of catastrophe. But could it have turned back and erased the years of concentrated work and research? The children of the survivors of the *pikadon** retain the memory of the sky turned into a crater and of people who flew away with the light and turned into shadows. People are not responsible for the past, but they live in the present and create the future. Whatever decision you may make, remember that you are creating your children's future."

The ensuing stillness was broken only by the hum of the computers. Multicolored lights ran along their panels, forming constellations, breaking apart, flickering and uncaring.

Erik's speech was perhaps the shortest.

"We do not have the right to destroy the biotosis physically, because no one can predict the aftereffects of such an action. We are tied to the World Soul, and the death of the biotosis may cause serious psychological trauma for the entire world. Thus the path to the liquidation of the unwanted influence of the biotosis lies in long research of the properties and characteristics of the development of this biological formation."

Erik glanced at his watch. The recess was over. It was time to go back into the auditorium. He got up and limped back to the entrance.

---

* Japanese: The entire complex of aftereffects of an atomic blast.

Chapter 9

ERIK WAS TIRED. Tired of councils, meetings, and press conferences.
He had had his fill of the foreigners' languages—barking,
burbling, rustling babble—and of the large chandelier in the
Palace of Science. Its steady swaying brought on centrifugal day-
dreaming in Erik: his surroundings spun faster and faster until
they disappeared and Erik was left alone in the huge dark auditorium. Only Ermolov's deep voice could penetrate Erik's daze.

And they finally did come to a conclusion. They had probably
done all they could. But that was precisely what Erik considered
wrong. They presented their decision on three closely typed pages
and tried to leave nothing out. The main conclusion was to find
a way to liquidate the biotosis. True, it was recommended that
this be done after preliminary research into the properties and
attributes of the amazing polymer, but one way or another, the

biotosis was judged to be harmful. There were close to a thousand biologists, chemists, physicists, and philosophers in the special international commission. This army of people who could barely understand one another were expected to analyze the biotosis and all the possible social, economic, and psychological consequences of its existence.

Erik could only shake his head when he first saw the commission in full array. The room was filled with people—young and old, bald and curly-haired, black, white, and brown. A tall ship travels far, thought Erik, but very slowly. The thought did not leave him during the endless speeches on minor organizational matters. When it was Erik's turn to speak, he said:

"We've lost too much time evaluating the situation. I'm afraid it's irretrievable. The biotosis is developing and the tempo of its development is unprecedented. It's growing, increasing in volume, perfecting itself. Its development does not cease for a second. Our statistics show that the distance at which EMO now takes effect is decreasing and the force of EMO is increasing. This means that the source of radiation—in this case the biotosis—is returning the signals it receives from people more and more accurately and powerfully. The biotosis is developing by leaps and bounds. What the next leap will bring we have no way of predicting. It could be the most unexpected thing. Therefore we must try to complete our planned studies as quickly as possible. We must find a way of isolating the biotosis or undertake the usual . . . methods of liquidation."

Erik's speech seemed to have an effect. But then there were thirty other speeches in support of his suggestion for speeding up the research, and he decided to escape from this Tower of Babel.

He lived near a pool. He could see its thin shell stretched over aluminum ribs from his open window. The green water, the white stones of the artificial beach, and the tanned bathers showed through the shell. In the morning, Erik would sit on the windowsill and use an electromassage brush on his knee. The skin would turn a purplish red. The videophone had been disconnected a long time ago, and he could devote himself entirely to the pleasures of the massage. The motor hummed pleasantly. Brightly colored aerobuses flew past his window, merry faces behind their windows. A boy downstairs threw a pebble into an open ground-floor window and hid in the courtyard from an angry red-faced fat woman.

Life went on. It seemed that no one was even thinking about the biotosis. Even he thought about it less and less. The biotosis was no longer his; it was naked, and thousands of strangers' eyes were looking at it. It wasn't that Erik was vain or jealous, but for some reason he did not like thinking about the biotosis any more—as though the biopolymer had not lived up to his expectations, had failed some very important test.

Once in a while, Erik dropped in on Sergei's father. Arefyev senior had not changed much since his son's disappearance, but he seemed bleaker. They sat quietly, had coffee, smoked. Sometimes Erik told him about the commission's work or about the biotosis. Arefyev senior smoked his pipe and shook his head, and it was never clear whether he agreed with Erik or not.

Ermolov called in Erik.

"The commission is ready to set off for Khokai-Rokh."

Erik nodded.

"You will go with the first party."

"All right."

He went home happy. There was no trace of his depression.

He got to the airport early. The day was cold and gray. The members of the commission were dressed in black and gray plastic raincoats. But Erik was carefree. He found the harsh cold air invigorating and his fellow travelers terrific guys.

Ermolov, who was there to see them off, frowned when he saw Erik's elation.

"Don't go off half-cocked. Be serious."

They said their goodbyes warmly. The aerobuses flew up into the air.

Khokai-Rokh looked like a fortified region from the days of the last world war. Erik laughed aloud when he saw the ditch dug around the biotosis, the barbed wire, and the radar installations.

"You have a fertile imagination," he said to Khokhrin, the director of the camp. "Do you really think that the biotosis might run off?"

"To ensure against any possible aggression," the embarrassed fat man explained.

Khokhrin had been the director of a major zoo. Erik was mystified as to why such a man had been entrusted with organizing the first scientific studies of the biotosis. Maybe someone associated the biotosis with wild bears. But that was no basis for an important administrative decision.

The first party consisted of one hundred and twenty scientists. Erik knew about fifteen of them by name and could recognize another twenty or so. He did not know the others and had never heard anything about them. But they all knew him, and that simplified things a bit.

"Where will we put them all?" he asked Oleg Zaozersky, a well-known young biochemist, named head of the first party.

"Don't worry! Everything's been prepared. Look." He pointed to the buildings erected at the foot of the biotosis. Erik couldn't recognize the biostation where he and Sergei had spent so many anxious moments. The building had grown in width and height. It was an entire research institute now. In the yard there were several shacks, crowned with antennas and air-conditioning ducts. Erik peeked into one of the shacks and saw white-coated lab workers, microscopes, and X-ray equipment. Lacquered and chromed, the instruments of science saluted their leader. Erik pursed his lips but said nothing.

The arrivals dropped their elegant luggage, bags, and boxes of equipment and hurried over to the biotosis. Erik and Zaozersky stayed back and walked slowly along the moat. As Erik walked he thought that the biotosis had changed little since the last time he had seen it.

Except that the odor was stronger. What was that gas? He wondered if anyone had thought to analyze it.

"The World Soul. How wonderful," he heard someone say.

Erik glanced at Zaozersky in amazement. His eyes were glistening moistly and his pale face registered unfeigned awe.

The biotosis was truly beautiful. The magnificent giant flower lay on the ground, its firm petals opened up to the sky. It glowed with a cool, shimmering light. And the light was alive.

They're falling in love with the biotosis, Erik thought. They all will. After all, it's so beautiful. But . . . it's like that fat director said. We're all living on a volcano here.

He examined the biotosis carefully and suddenly realized that it had changed. His worries had not been for nothing. The biotosis had not only grown in size. It had changed. The flabby, lumpy parts were gone, and the dark chasms on its slopes were gone, too. The World Soul was now perfectly shaped. There was nothing superfluous in it. There seemed to be perfect harmony in its form.

The scientists returned from their examination of the biotosis subdued and abashed. It was clear to everyone now that they had to move carefully and thoughtfully. Very carefully.

"That director isn't as dumb as we thought at first," Zaozersky said, looking through his reports. "He hasn't done one stupid thing in relation to the biotosis. And that's pretty smart."

"You mean, all those barbed-wire fences and barriers are to protect the biotosis from people and not the other way around?" Erik asked.

"Right. He's guarding the biotosis from birds and rodents and insects and parasites. In dry spells, he's even watered it."

"I see. Who told him to do that?"

"His own initiative. But you'd better talk to him."

Zaozersky greeted the director.

"Petr Mikhailovich, who suggested you water the biotosis?"

"Well, you know, it just seems calmer that way. When it was baking in the sun, I felt bad. And this way it feels good and people feel better, too."

"I see. Thank you."

Erik and Zaozersky exchanged a look. Erik smiled and the biochemist just sighed.

"All right, let's have a look at what science has done."

For the next five hours Zaozersky and his people went over the data gathered by the small group of scientists who had moved to Khokai-Rokh even before the arrival of the first party. They were headed by the Soviet biophysicist Tutorsky. They had managed to do an enormous amount of work on studying the biotosis' properties. But their work seemed to be missing something important. Perhaps because the director had not given them permission to perform any direct tests on the polymer. He

followed to the letter paragraph 17 of the temporary instruction
on dealing with the biopolymer. It forbade experimentation.
The strangest part was that when Erik read through the instruc-
tions, there was no paragraph 17.

"Tutorsky has simplified our task tremendously. We won't
have to perform a whole pack of unnecessary experiments. We'll
set up our equipment tomorrow and get right down to the
basics," Zaozersky said.

Thanks to the work of Tutorsky's group they did not have to
study the dynamics of volume changes, or photograph the fluctu
ations in the biotosis' light, or determine the intensity of the
exchange of gases. Zaozersky could proceed immediately to the
biopotentials of the polymer. The experiment was simple. Eight
silver plates with wires soldered to them were placed on different
parts of the biotosis. They were weighted for better contact.
Erik was worried while he placed the electrodes. But everything
went well.

All the measuring equipment was set up on the other side of
the moat. Erik was exhausted from crawling around the slippery
petals of the biotosis.

Mopping his brow, he said to Zaozersky, "It's a frightening
thing, the biotosis."

"Why?"

"Just is. Frightening."

They said nothing. Each thought his own thoughts. But there
wasn't any time for standing around thinking. The experiment
showed that the biotosis had an intense electrical life. The current was unbelievably strong for a material of that structure.

"Live matter can't carry a current like this," said Surenoga, a
biophysicist, as he looked over the graphs.

Someone else added, "There should be copper wires running
through it."

The phenomenon of the anomalous current interested the
scientists, and they became engrossed in studying it. Khokhrin
circled the biotosis, following the researchers who were putting
more electrodes on the polymer.

"For God's sake, take it easy!" he shouted from below, as
though the electrodes were being implanted on his naked heart.
"Hey you, mister, comrade, sir! Don't press so hard!"

Erik concentrated on processing the data. The picture emerging was interesting but incomprehensible. Zaozersky was interested in how the World Soul's biocurrents could be related to the mutual overlay effect. Despite the vast amount of data they had, the connection, if it existed at all, remained obscure.

"What's the matter?" Zaozersky asked Erik.

They were on the terrace watching the Italians play ping-pong. The best player turned out to be sixty-year-old Professor Terma. He was on the twelfth game of a winning streak.

"We have to decide," Erik replied. "First analysis, then synthesis. We have to analyze the biotosis. It has to be cut. Only when we understand the structure of the polymer can we hope to understand its functions. Everything else is just a waste of time."

"But that was attempted once, wasn't it? Unsuccessfully?"

"Yes, there was an attempt. But ... there were special circumstances. Arefyev might have been wrong, after all."

"It must be very dangerous."

"I feel that way too, but I can't understand why. After all, what harm can it do to people?"

The question remained unanswered.

"How can it harm humanity, and us in particular?" asked the Hungarian chemist and philosopher Norka Derdi at the evening meeting. "We must try. If the biotosis experiments on people, why can't man reply in kind? Do we or don't we have the right to experiment?"

"It's not a question of rights," Zaozersky said. "We're talking about the possible repercussions of direct action on the biotosis. Have we any idea what we're dealing with?"

"It's a vicious circle! In order to know the biotosis, we have to analyze it. But in order to analyze it, we have to know what a biotosis is!" Surenoga laughed. An argument broke out. Erik was reminded of the endless debates at the Palace of Science.

"We'll try to get a specimen tomorrow," he said suddenly.

Even he had not expected to say that. But his authority as the creator of the World Soul was total. Zaozersky looked at Erik with interest.

"This experiment will have two aspects," Erik continued.

"First, the purely scientific. We must know what the biotosis is. And secondly, the social aspect. I'm referring to the autonomy of the biotosis. Is it actually capable of self-defense that poses a threat to mankind, or is it simply a blob of jelly? We must find out."

Erik's unilateral decision caused uncertainty and then a stormy discussion. But Erik knew that his words had relieved all the scientists present, including Zaozersky, the head of the party, of the burden of responsibility.

Before dawn Zaozersky dropped into Erik's room. The young scientist was sitting at the open window watching the glowing mass. His bed had not been slept in.

"Nervous?" Zaozersky asked.

"No," Erik said calmly. "I'm reminiscing. It turns out I have things to reminisce about."

The smoke from Erik's cigarette mingled with the fresh morning air coming through the window.

"What about Arefyev? Has he been found?" Zaozersky inquired.

"No."

"What happened to him? I've only heard rumors."

Erik was quiet. It was obviously painful for him to talk about it.

"Please don't think that I'm prying."

"I don't. It just happened. Sergei was very unstable. Very strong and very weak. In the situation in which he found himself, the blows fell on his weak spots."

After a moment, Erik continued.

"I miss him very much sometimes. Even though we didn't get along toward the end. But he. . . ."

Erik didn't finish, and Zaozersky said nothing more.

"So what about our experiment today?" Zaozersky spoke in a hearty voice. "Should we put it off, maybe?"

Erik looked at him.

"No," he said after some thought. "We must act. The experiment is inevitable anyway."

We must act!

The operation was to be carried out by robot AI-27. The light

little automaton looked like a schoolbag placed on narrow cater-
pillar tracks. The scientists at the control panel set up in the
field watched the robot with mixed feelings of anxiety and hope.
When it set off, Erik raised his hand as if to stop it, and then
shrugged, embarrassed. The engineer handling the machine looked
at Erik in surprise and turned away.

The robot moved smoothly along the dusty road, the chrome
of its joints gleaming in the sun. The sun was reflected in its
orange head. It's autumn in Moscow, Erik thought. The leaves
are falling. And it's still summer here.

He looked around, afraid someone might have heard his
thoughts. But they were all concentrating on the robot. Almost
the entire party that had come from Moscow was there, as well
as some of the custodial staff.

"There he goes, the bugger!" Khokhrin muttered.

The robot clambered up on top of the biotosis and hobbled
easily across the intricate patterns of the polymer. The robot
was approaching the section they wanted cut. They had picked
an area with the highest intensity of biocurrents.

Where's Dr. Karmin? Erik suddenly thought. Then he remembered; he was coming with the second party, with Ermolov.

"I'm giving the order," the engineer said and pushed the key.
And immediately fell from his seat.

Erik heard the scream first and then felt the pain. But before
the pain came, there was a split second during which he saw
the people next to him falling and running. Distorted faces, flut-
tering lab coats, convulsed bodies hung frozen in the air. Terma
tearing at his collar, Zaozersky, mouth open wide, screaming.
Khokhrin bounded into the steppe with rabbitlike leaps.

Then the pain. Erik fell, got up, then fell again. He saw
nothing now. When he had crawled over to the controls, the
clouds in his eyes were shattering into millions of sparks. Erik
couldn't find the right key at first. He hit all of them at once.
The robot exploded, but Erik didn't hear it happen.

He was unconscious for less than two minutes. The dust raised
by the feet of the runners had not yet settled. There was no
robot on the biotosis. Erik got up, leaning on the metal supports
of the control panel. Someone was moaning. Erik saw the engineer struggling to get up. The scientists were returning from the

steppe, tired and dirty. Two of them were carrying the body of the Italian.

"Terma is dead," Khokhrin said sadly.

Erik told them to put the professor on the ground. He listened to his heart. It wasn't beating.

One after another, the scientists left for the biostation. No one spoke. Workmen came and took away the control panel on a low flat dolly. Erik watched distractedly. He didn't feel bad. In fact, he felt good; there wasn't a trace of the pain left in his body. He thought that it was time for him to be going too. A clear and strong desire to leave overwhelmed him. He looked around in amazement. What was he doing there? He was letting down a team of excellent people. They needed a biochemist there! He had to leave immediately. He hurried to the biostation, pulling off his lab coat as he went.

The station was bustling with activity. Workers, lab assistants, and mechanics scurried about with a busy look, getting ready for the trip. A rainbow pile of luggage was stacked up in the lobby. Strangers arrived from somewhere, laid Professor Terma into a zinc coffin, and took him away. The professor's countrymen accompanied the body to the aerobus stop. When they came back they redoubled their efforts to pack.

Erik was packed when Zaozersky came up to him. He had been watching Erik's hurried and precise movements.

"I'm staying," Zaozersky said.

"Here?"

"Yes."

Erik locked his suitcase and tightened the strap.

"Well, good luck," he said, shaking Zaozersky's hand.

"I was glad to meet you."

As Erik was leaving, Zaozersky shouted after him.

"Listen!"

Erik came back.

"Wouldn't you like to. . . ."

"To stay here with you?"

"Well, yes." Zaozersky made a face and smoothed his throat as though something were blocking his air.

Erik smiled.

"Are you kidding? They're waiting for me!"

Zaozersky laughed.

"Of course, of course. Go ahead."

There weren't enough cars, and there was a crowd at the bus stop. People smoked, joked, and gabbed. When the next aerobus pulled up, no one moved. The bus parked and opened its doors.

"Everybody in."

Then some people detached themselves from the crowd and slowly moved toward the steps. Erik let them through. He knew that they had to leave even more than he did. Maybe they were waiting for them more than for him.

"The next one isn't for twenty minutes," a merry young voice said next to him. It was Surenoga.

"Going far?"

"Home to Bucharest."

The next bus came and Erik was getting on it when someone pointed to the horizon and asked:

"Look, what's that?"

The World Soul lay on the earth, black against the setting sun.

"What do you mean? It's the biotosis!" Erik replied.

When Erik got back to Moscow, he headed straight for the suburb of Kuntsevo, without even stopping at his apartment. He strolled down the wide, lively street, brightly lit with mercury-vapor lamps. The street was called Lunnyi Prospect and it led down to the Moscow River. Just before the wide marble steps that went down to the embankment, Erik turned toward a tall building hidden in the depths of a dark courtyard. The huge windows on all the floors were lit with an even milky light.

Erik left his suitcase in the vestibule and went up to the third floor. People in white lab coats were waiting for him in the large, airy room. A young woman took him into a room that sparkled with an array of snow-white sinks, mirrors, and chrome-plated fixtures. Erik scrubbed up, then smeared his hands with iodine. When he was ready they helped him into an outfit that revealed only his eyes and took him down a long corridor.

"Is this the patient?" Erik asked, indicating a long object covered with sheets.

"Yes."

Fifteen minutes later Erik had finished the analysis of the

growth. It was benign. Erik left the operating room. The surgeon began sewing up the incision.

Erik, exhausted, was barely able to stand on his feet and he didn't have the strength to get away from a woman who rushed toward him in the lobby. She babbled words of gratitude, tears streaming down her face. Erik sank into a chair and looked at her in surprise.

"Why are you telling me all this? I'm just doing my job, and besides, I'm not the surgeon."

The woman said, "I wanted to make you feel good. But...."

She looked crestfallen and went to sit in a corner.

They took Erik to an apartment. He was very sleepy and he saw the new autumn day coming through his delicious sleepiness. People were running to their cars. Erik followed the bright colors of their clothes with his eyes. He could see the blue splashes of the puddles and he could hear the whoosh of passing cars. A feeling of peace and deep satisfaction came to him. It was like a confident expectation of happiness.

The apartment they had for Erik was small and comfortable. Erik fell asleep as soon as he got into the large bed.

Thus began a quiet and monotonous period in Erik's life. But he didn't seem to notice that he should have been bored. He assisted at operations, analyzed the results, getting better at it with every passing day. At home in the evenings he studied medical books and learned many things. He met many people, exercised, went to plays. He sent taped letters to his parents in Odessa regularly. They sent back quiet, lecturing answers. He loved to put the tapes in the machine and watch his parents' faces and listen to their voices. The old people, as usual, were worried by something and tried to keep any real or imagined problems from their darling son. Erik tried to soothe them, telling them in detail about his work and his dissertation, which he had begun writing. He was advancing at work. He was developing original diagnostic methods and felt that every victory cleared the path for other, even more brilliant ones.

Then something disrupted his workaday life. One night, just before dawn, he jumped out of bed in extreme agitation. He dressed quickly and ran out into the street. The first snow of the year had fallen the week before, but it had melted. Black pud-

dles glistened in the dark. There was a damp wind. The street
lamps, dimmed for the night, shone dully. Ragged smoky clouds
raced above the rooftops.

People were running down the street. There were a lot of
silent running figures, dressed haphazardly, but they did not run
into one another or get in one another's way. They were all
headed in the same direction, running down the marble steps.

Erik saw red reflections. A multistoried building was burning
on the other bank. Erik recognized it. It was a boarding school.
He screamed and ran to the school.

"I'm not surprised that we saved the children," Erik said the
next day to his neighbor. He was examining his torn slippers.
"But why didn't I catch cold? Nine hours with wet, bare feet."

"Nervous excitement. There are no colds in wartime."

"That's true. But at least a runny nose?"

Before that event, he had often gone into the gray wintry
park to lose himself in the cold, wet paths and watch the Moscow River sleep in its red granite casing. He might stand on the
new bridge in the hot, fast wake of the electric buses.

But now he wanted to experience something strong and unexpected. Filling out reports and seeing the chief surgeon's hand-
writing made him sick. He felt confused, unsteady, nervous. A
pain in his heart came and went in waves, leaving regret and
anticipation of the next attack.

Erik left the hospital quickly. The automatic street-cleaning
machines were clearing the snow. The dirty asphalt, like a torn
leopard skin, shone with thousands of brilliant sparkles. A mi-
raculously preserved oak leaf blazed red in the sunshine. Erik
heard a familiar melody in the chaotic noise of the street. Three
aerobuses whizzed by one after another. That wasn't it! Someone
praised the weather and clicked shut his umbrella. That wasn't
it! There were baskets of apples on the corner of Chernyshev
Prospect. They had a sweet, almost elusive, beckoning smell. But
that wasn't it either!

It was a melody hopelessly lost in the hustle and bustle of the
crowds, the noise of the city, the shimmer of the sky.

Then Erik saw a door. Rather, he saw a building with a door
in it. It was right between the Bolshoi Department Store and a

taxi stand. The buildings around it were shiny and modern, but its door was old and ugly, a hopelessly outmoded door. And there was a handpainted sign over it. That was really sweet and touching. It was a short and simple sign: "Sardine Café." Erik pushed the door open and went in. He went down a few steps and through a narrow passageway to a large, dim room. The light curtains on the barred windows were hand-painted with fish, shrimp, and starfish. Erik took a table and looked around. The room was made to look like a grotto on the bottom of the sea. Lobsters crawled along the walls, and seaweed, hiding tiny marine life, swayed at his feet. There was a pale-green light at the exit, leading to the bar, a sunken ship covered with barnacles and seaweed. Transparent tinkling music came from the corner of the room. Erik was all alone in the strange room, and he felt uncomfortable.

He got up.

"Don't go, I'll be right with you," said a low voice.

A light went on over the entrance, and the drawing of the octopus moved. A little man, pale, gray-haired and gray-skinned, floated up to Erik.

"What would you like to order?"

The man was gentle and kind. There was something pleading and expectant in his voice. The melody of the past, the melody of forgetfulness rang in Erik's ears again. He had to reconstruct something familiar and dear from the ruins and ashes. It was exhausting, unnatural work. Real self-torture.

"All right," Erik finally said. He tried to wave his thoughts away. "Bring me a bottle of cognac."

The man moved off happily. His bluish cheeks were suffused with a rosy glow and his eyes brightened in gratitude. He was gone.

Erik looked after him in surprise. His energetic urgency ruined the effect of the dreamy swaying of the linen waves. But perhaps that was the way to behave in this Blue Grotto that was called the Sardine for some reason.

"Let's go," the man said touching Erik's arm.

"Where to?"

"There, where you'll be drinking." He pointed to the barnacled ship.

Erik went to the room. There was a cleverly decorated bar on the ship. Erik sat on a stool, facing the bottles and glasses arrayed on a glass counter.

"I'll leave you now," said the white little man. "Please help yourself. You'll find everything you need for the most refined tastes. Thank you."

He went out the back door into the dark hallway. Erik picked up a bottle. It was dusty. He ran his finger over it. The label fell off in a dark-brown powder. Erik opened the bottle with a rusty corkscrew and poured out the golden-brown liquid into his glass. He drank three shots in a row, corked the bottle, and put it back among its dirty and dusty mates.

Someone came in. His step was free and light. A person used to walking. Erik could hear his deep heavy breathing. The newcomer sat at the bar next to Erik. He took one of the bottles with a swift, sure movement and poured the clear liquid into his glass. Erik kept looking at his profile, listening to the melody of his lost past. The stranger finished his drink and turned to Erik.

"You haven't been here before. Where did you come from?"

Erik kept staring at him. He thought that his heart was about to stop.

"Why won't you talk?" the stranger asked and reached for another bottle.

Erik looked into his eyes and said, "I know you."

"Oh, I see. . . . Well, why not? We all know each other nowadays. But tell me, what brought you to this dump? Nobody seems to notice it."

Erik's tension eased. The melody got softer. It didn't die, no, but it was too low and too far away to hear.

The stranger smiled.

"I see, you just dropped in by accident. It happens," he said abruptly. "They call me the Captain, and I come here almost every day."

"Why?"

The Captain thought.

"I come here to understand why I come here. That's stupid. Just sophistry in the final analysis, elementary tautology. But . . . that really is it. When I understand that, I'll understand everything."

Erik rubbed his temples.

"But why ... why do you seem so familiar to me? Captain, tell me, who did you used to be? What's your name?"

"My name is Sergei Arefyev. Why, does it mean anything to you?"

Erik shook his head.

"No."

"That's what I mean. I would give a lot to meet someone who knew me."

The little old man showed up among the shells and netting.

"Are my customers happy? Are you satisfied?"

"Fine, fine," the Captain said. "Go on now."

The old man left slowly.

"And what's your name?"

"Erik Erdman. Why do you treat him like that?"

"Erik ... Erdman," the Captain repeated, playing with his glass. "Yes, I know the name, the way I know Don Quixote or Einstein. But unlike the other names, yours is empty, like my glass."

He thought some more and shook his head.

"No, I don't know you, I don't. So, let's drink to our acquaintance."

"No. I won't have any more to drink."

"As you like, but I will."

Chapter 10

KARABICHEV FELT that he had done enough. He wanted only one thing—to get back to Moscow as fast as possible. He nagged his doctors, as though they could speed his healing process. He did manage to get his own way. They let him out early. It was a mistake.

The first cool evening breeze knocked Karabichev off his feet. He was taken with double pneumonia to another, unfamiliar hospital. He had almost no money left, and Professor Rioli was paying for him. That tall, calm man found time in his heavy schedule to visit Karabichev regularly.

When Karabichev, stuffed to the gills with antibiotics, started getting better, Rioli began bringing him news from the outside world along with the usual fruit. So Karabichev learned of the birth of the World Soul, its creators, and the extremely urgent congress of scientists devoted to the biotosis. Rioli brought him photographs of Khokai-Rokh, showed him pictures of Sergei and Erik reprinted in the local paper from Soviet, British, and German newspapers.

Karabichev was too weak for conversation, but he listened rapturously to Señor Rioli's smooth, steady speech.

"I was wrong, of course," the professor said, "but that's not the point. The appearance of this invention is not accidental. Thousands of barriers were overcome in creating the biotosis, no?"

Karabichev nodded.

"And therefore, its appearance is not accidental, but necessary, no?"

Karabichev said nothing.

"You probably won't agree with me, but I will go so far as to say that it was preordained," Rioli said uncertainly.

Karabichev smiled.

"Preordained by the development of human society. People needed the biotosis, and it appeared. When people needed the steam engine, it was invented, no? And now people are running an experiment on man as society."

Karabichev laughed.

"As soon as I get out of here, I'll answer all your points!"

"I'll be very happy to hear you. Do you know my basic premise? I repeat: In order for our society to become humane, every member must change and in many ways lose human traits —at least as we understand the term today."

"I know your premise."

Rioli left, and Karabichev watched after him. He remembered their long conversation about the horrible legless cripple. Rioli proved to him convincingly that in this case any attempts to understand would be fruitless. The cripple was mentally defective, and no other intellectual or emotional pattern could be imprinted clearly on that murky soul.

"I suppose," Rioli said then, "that your wife was broken into several . . . how shall I put it . . . shards. She gave a piece of her soul to many people, including that beggar. Stop your seeking. Go home. When everything quiets down, and time passes, your wife's material basis will reconstitute her former mental image. You have nothing to worry about. Learn to wait."

One evening when Karabichev was feeling better and already anticipating being released, something happened to him. He was lying in bed by the window and looking at the long narrow leaves of the unfamiliar trees.

Suddenly he experienced a momentary weakness and pain. He was scared. What is this? A relapse? he thought. But the pain overwhelming his body had nothing to do with the former dull ache of his illness. This pain covered him like a wave, and he whirled in its invisible eddies. Then it slid off slowly, leaving a delicious languor in his body. The sweat on Karabichev's brow dried and color came to his cheeks. And Karabichev realized that the wave of pain was draining away the important part of his life. His "I" was floating away; the pain had drawn out his essence from mysterious depths and crannies. And now there was something on the hospital bed that was named Andrei Karabichev, but which had a very remote connection to him.

"The World Soul? But why?" Terror engulfed Karabichev. He jumped out of bed.

"I don't want it," he shouted.

His voice echoed hollowly in the empty room. Then the terror passed. Karabichev felt tranquil and good. Had he been sick, hanging around in this bed for over a month? What nonsense! He had to go. Karabichev dressed and left.

Karabichev walked down the street from the hospital. He knew its name: the Blue Arrow. Blue because it went down to the sea, Arrow because it was Bessano's only straight street. He wanted a smoke and got his matches, but he couldn't find his cigarettes. They must have been taken away by the hospital. Rummaging through his pockets, he came across his passport, opened it, and saw his photograph.

He remembered Maria, his Moscow apartment, the old videophone in the hall, the Institute of Telepathy, the World Soul, Ermolov, Sergei—everything in color, moving, alive. There was something else, vague, but warm, familiar, and exciting. Karabichev tried to clear up that dark blurred memory, but the pain, unbearable and wild, engulfed him once more. He was doubled over by it. His whole body ached—his skin, his eyes, and even his hair. Karabichev put away the passport with his pain-stiffened fingers and went down the Blue Arrow. He turned off into a square, went around the town hall, and found himself in a large old courtyard. There were several others there, dressed in old, worn clothing. Strange people, suspicious looks, quick, agile movements.

They heard sharp, military footsteps, and an old priest in a cassock appeared from a dark archway, accompanied by two young men carrying boxes. Karabichev got closer. The priest blessed them and began his sermon. His speech was like a dream for Karabichev, fading in and out of his understanding.

The priest spoke of the lofty mission that had fallen on the shoulders of those present, spoke of the goodness and peace in which all mankind was living, and about God's laws, which had become universal. "And if you are entrusted with such somber work in these holy times, have faith—it must be done for the people! The ones you will kill have been marked by the devil. They are the enemies of humanity's body and soul. Let your hand be steady and your soul know no doubts!"

Karabichev examined the men around him and thought that they had never known and would probably never know any doubt. They were given pistols and extra ammunition. Then they dispersed, without a farewell or a backward glance.

Karabichev remembered very well how pleasant it was to hold the gun in his hands and how he liked the shiny gray barrel and the black textured handle. But everything else was clouded.

Karabichev did not remember where he was living when he threw away the useless gun. Time had stopped for him.

One day he was wandering down a dark, crooked street. The cobblestones looked oiled in the moonlight. Three tall men walked out of a café. They talked and laughed, shook hands, and separated. The tallest one started down the steps that led to the wharf, and soon dissolved in the black shadows. His heavy shoes rang hollowly in the dark. The other two asked Karabichev for a light. Karabichev patted his pockets and shrugged.

There was a shot below, followed by a muffled moan. The two men ran in the direction of the shot before Karabichev realized what it was. He followed.

He found them bent over the man who had left alone. He was sitting up, leaning against a rickety fence. In the leafy shadows of the trees, Karabichev saw him holding his shoulder with his left hand.

"Did you see what those bastards are doing? Hah? They're getting ready for a fascist putsch!" one of the men said to Karabichev. "They've been terrorizing the south and now they're moving up here. Well, we'll show them."

"Is he in a lot of pain?" Karabichev asked.

"Remember one thing, pal. As long as you feel pain, you're a man!" the wounded man said.

Looking at the pale, contorted face, Karabichev had an insight. The man was in terrible pain. Probably pain a thousand times worse than what Andrei Karabichev felt. And he wore his pain like a badge, an invisible proud banner. In the name of what? The struggle. And there it was. That was the indicator of consciousness. Pain! As long as it sears your body, you maintain consciousness, you think, you remain yourself. Today escape into happiness and peace is a step toward moral weakness.

Pain—there's your life preserver, Andrei. Hold onto it with both hands, hold on tight, sink your teeth into it, don't ever let go, or else . . . or else some unknown force will rock you in the ripples of well-being and smugness, and you will cease to be a man.

Karabichev walked down the hot streets. What am I doing here? Who am I?

Karabichev divided all his subsequent feelings into two categories: enlightenment and oblivion. Enlightenment was accompanied by waves of pain that led to dizziness and unconsciousness; oblivion, by delicious, intoxicating languor. The former was filled with sharp, bright impressions. Oblivion forever remained a mystery for Karabichev. It was always accompanied by the feeling of a calm, deep self-confidence. It bordered on joy, but there was something muddy and vague about it. Like looking through a rain-washed window at cars and passersby. Rivulets and drops distorted outlines, disfigured lines and colors, and made everything blurred, smeared, and nameless.

Winter finally came to Khokai-Rokh. Heavy sticky snow fell and melted. And fell again and melted again. The hot living earth battled with the cold sky, and oily rivers poured from the battlefield and a blue thick fog rose into the air.

"It's like pea soup," Karabichev said to his companions, as his greedy eyes tried to break through the fog that enveloped the valley.

His companions said nothing. The pale, serious men, women, and teenagers who filled the heavy long-distance aerobus were lost in themselves and their tense anticipation.

"Visibility is zero," said the driver. "We're landing blind."

They landed safely not far from the station. The silent building stared at them gloomily with its blind, darkened windows.

"You can't see the biotosis!" someone said.

"The fog is too thick. Well, let's go," Karabichev said.

They picked up their bags and splashed through the mud to the station. A woman stopped and pointed.

"Look, look!"

She was pointing at a fresh mound of dirt. Dark streams of water poured along its muddy sides. There was a pole with a sign nailed to it clumsily stuck at the top.

"It's a grave . . . a fresh one."

Karabichev bent closer.

"I can't make it out. The ink is blurred. 'Here lies. . . .' No, I can't tell. All right, let's go, we'll find out later."

It was empty and cold in the station yard. The doors of the house were ajar. Pieces of board and wire were scattered on the front steps. There was a strange contraption in a corner of the yard. It looked like a large radio telescope. The snow had wet the latticed reflector, which was approximately five feet in diameter, and it sparkled with a thousand red beads arranged in a spiral.

"Why, those are ruby crystals! That's interesting. Why is the thing here?"

"And it's been worked on recently. Look, Andrei, the contacts have been cleaned," an elderly man said, pointing out the cable attached to the switchboard.

"Yes, and this wire will lead us to them."

They entered the house Indian-file. They were greeted by silence, empty rooms, dusty equipment, mildewed walls, and clutter.

"Hear that?" Karabichev stopped, raising his hand. They all

froze. There was a faraway hammering. "Tap-tap-tap-tap."

"Movement!" Karabichev strode forward confidently.

There was a light on in one of the rooms on the second floor. Karabichev pulled on the door. It squeaked and opened.

There were no windows in the room. The walls and ceiling were covered by long rows of wires twisted into spirals, with tiny ruby crystals swaying on them. Various sprockets and electronic parts were strewn around the room. There were three beds along the walls, and a man was sleeping on one of them. His feet, in dirty nylon socks, stuck out over the edge. A desk was squeezed into a corner, and a man was writing at the desk. The desk lamp projected his tousled hair onto the wall as a huge fluffy cloud. The man didn't hear the door squeak or Karabichev's heavy, careful breathing. His hand was racing along the yellow pages of a laboratory journal.

Karabichev coughed. The man jumped up. He was a slight, unshaven, pale man in glasses. There was horror in his eyes.

"Oleg!" he called hoarsely.

The sleeping man sat up. "Who's this?" he asked, looking at Karabichev and his group in surprise.

"What do you want?" the man with glasses demanded.

Karabichev took a step toward him.

"Forgive the intrusion, friends. We came without advance notice. But what can you do, we had to. Perhaps we should get acquainted first?"

Oleg had been sleeping fully clothed. He got up, shoved his feet into his slippers, and said, "Why not, let's get acquainted."

The man who had been writing withdrew into the corner. His glasses flashed fearfully behind the potentiometer.

"The atmosphere in here is completely different," Karabichev said, extending his hand to Oleg. "It's easier to breathe in here, freer, I guess—"

Oleg sprang away from him.

"None of that! No shaking hands! Just tell me your name."

Karabichev dropped his hand in embarrassment.

"Andrei Anatolyevich Karabichev," he said softly.

The others had come into the room and were standing around him.

There was a movement behind the equipment. The man

came out of hiding and stopped within three feet of Karabichev.

"Where do you work now?" he asked. His voice was harsh and commanding.

"I don't work."

"Where did you work at the beginning of the year?"

"At the Institute of Telepathy, as senior scientist."

"Oleg, do you hear? He remembers everything. I know him!" The man in glasses was overjoyed.

"Why did you come here?"

Karabichev said nothing. The tension was mounting. Lightning was about to strike. And it did.

"Erik, is that you?" a hoarse deep voice asked. A middle-aged, gray-haired man came out of the group.

"Ermolov? Are you here, too?"

"Yes, yes, I am. We are all completely normal, healthy people. We remember, we remember everything and understand everything. But it's not easy. But how about you?"

Ermolov's voice shook. The barrier was broken and the people were hugging, filling the room with exclamations, jokes, and laughter.

"And we were afraid!" Erik said. "You can expect almost anything from the biotosis. You don't even trust yourself nowadays, not to mention strangers."

"I would have recognized you right away if it weren't for the beard."

"I'd like you to meet Oleg Zaozersky, a biochemist, the only one to withstand the World Soul," Erik said.

"Come on, Erik, don't be ridiculous!" Oleg protested.

"We came here to tear your biotosis to shreds!" Ermolov announced.

"How?"

"Wait a minute!" Erik shouted. There was silence. "How did you manage to get here?"

Ermolov came up to Erik.

"First pain, then through the reflexes to the consciousness.

"And it's still not easy. We're always under terrible pressure. It's easier in here," Karabichev said.

"That's the protection," said Erik, indicating the spirals sprinkled with ruby crystals. After a moment he showed them the papers scribbled over with an uneven hand.

"This is the plan, the attack plan."

"Protection? Arefyev's concentrator idea? And where is he? Did he disappear?" Ermolov was bursting with questions.

Erik clenched his jaw.

"That will take an extremely difficult and long explanation."

"All right, we'll put it off, if it's long. I've been looking for you everywhere, Erik. May I sit down" Ermolov sat on the bed.

"Yes, please, sit down, comrades. But we don't seem to have enough chairs." Erik looked around the room, as though seeing it for the first time.

They laughed. Easily, freely, enjoying their redemption from a horrible burden. For the first time in many days they did not feel the pain to which they had subjected themselves constantly. And for the first time in many days they could sit close to another human being and not worry about being swept away in some psychological whirlpool.

"You see, brothers, what's happened," Ermolov said, unraveling his muffler. "We're left without specialists. After that experiment, everyone who had the remotest connection with the biotosis was put out of commission. It blocked them."

"That was to be expected." Erik had regained his cool academic demeanor. "Oleg and I figured it out."

"Well?"

"It was a simple defense mechanism. The biotosis closed off specific cells, closed them off without thinking, without reasoning, like a computer. It has a feedback connection with all people. The attack showed it just which cells had to be closed off. And it did it."

"More than that," Zaozersky added. "It questioned them, too."

"What questions?" Karabichev asked.

"Our consciousness is an open book to it."

"So?"

"That's a strange question." Zaozersky shrugged. "From Erik it found out about you, Ermolov, and dozens of people with whom he had a psychological connection. And it questioned them, too, and then blocked them. Thus it closed off the net, so to speak, getting thousands of people along the way with no connection to the operation. Relatives, friends."

"We thought it was something like that," Ermolov said.

"Who's 'we'?" Erik asked.

"The Extraordinary Committee."

"There is one?"

"You poor hicks," Ermolov said, "do you really think you're the only ones out here, alone and forgotten, saving humanity? It would be a bad day for humanity if its fate depended only on your efforts. We figured that the biotosis was cutting out people mechanically. Then we determined that its influence does not extend beyond the earth's biosphere. The rest was easy. A satellite with warheads is awaiting the signal to attack. The UN approved the measure unanimously in view of the extreme situation. If you only knew what was going on in the world! There are lots of people happy to fish in muddied waters. It makes life almost unlivable, what those bastards are up to."

"I know, I saw it," Karabichev said softly.

"What could you see in Bessano? There are worse things going on. Erik, that's the problem."

"Then what are you waiting for? Destroy it!" Zaozersky shook his fist in the air.

"We would have a long time ago. We have delayed because we don't know what the effect will be psychologically. The biotosis blocked out all the specialists. There's no one to confer with. We're looking for them all over the place, getting our people together."

"But they're not all . . . the way Oleg and I are. In working condition?" Erik said.

"That's no problem! As long as they're alive. We send them up to the satellite and they get back to normal quickly," Ermolov explained.

And they all laughed again, friendly, happy laughter.

"So everything that we did here was a waste." Zaozersky waved his hand around the room.

"What do you mean, a waste? You're marvelous people. You think I don't know from my own experience what it cost you to remain yourselves? For nothing? You're heroes! And I'm not

even talking about your protection. That will be important! ...
Too bad that Arefyev isn't here. We could take him to Moscow
and confer and then get to work. We can't waste any more
time. We have a few ideas, but we'll talk about it later. Where
is Sergei, Erik?"

"There is no more Sergei. This is all that's left of him." Erik
took a small cassette from his pocket. "He recorded it shortly
before he died."

THE TAPE OF SERGEI AREFYEV'S VOICE

I stayed away from home for two or three weeks. At first I
spent the night on park benches and in airport waiting rooms.
Then I went out into the country. That saved me. If I had
stayed in the city a few more days, I don't know what would
have happened to me.

I got off at Svetloe. A flat green field with a few birches open
to the sun and wind. A cheery forest, dressed in autumn hues,
stood on the horizon.

I jumped off into the leaf-filled gully and headed for the
forest. I walked quickly and energetically, even though I had no
reason to hurry.

I felt tired and lay down on the grass. It smelled of fresh hay.
The air was clean and crisp. I looked up. The sky was a chintz
tent and the sun a black hole. Why does the sun shine on the
earth? Why does it do it? I thought.

I heard some songbird's call. The simple melody melted into
the sun's rays. The wind, coming from the forest, caressed me
and whispered to me I tried to understand its language, but it
kept changing to a mumbled, good-natured murmur. I fell asleep
with the sun warm on my face. I slept long and deep and woke
only toward morning, when the sky was beginning to pale and
the stars had dissolved in the sky like sugar in milk. Chilled, I
warmed up by running around the meadow and slapping my
arms and shoulders.

I don't remember what happened to me next very well. There
were many bright moments and sharp sensations, but their con-
tinuity is erased from my mind, and I can't tell which came first
or last.

I remember myself in the forest, which was full of mushrooms. Their caps showed red on the meadow, like drops of blood shed by a magical beast. I cut open their fat, firm bodies and watched them turn blue when exposed to the air. I found them in the shadows of old pine trees, in the thick grass, in ditches along the road. The mushrooms didn't seem to have a favorite spot. Little boletuses winked at me from thick underbrush. The sticky purplish skin on their caps hid the delicate yellow tissue that resembled the fuzz of newly hatched chicks. The stately white-caps were as firm and flexible as wet wood.

I liked the tree mushrooms best. They formed bouquets on old stumps. Their delicate ears broke off easily, releasing an incomparable mushroom aroma. When I was very hungry, I made myself mushroom *assortis*. I would clean and chop the mushrooms fine, wrap them in leaves and clay, and bury them in a pit. Then I would light a fire over them. After thirty or forty minutes, I would break the clay crust and pick out the steaming mushrooms.

I once came across an ancient mushroom under a birch. Its mossy cap had formed a concave vase. Rainwater had collected in it, with pine needles and leaves floating on top. I drank the water and saw clouds near my lips. It felt as if I were drinking in the sky. It was tasteless and cool.

Then the horrible lapses in my memory came, when I wanted nothing.

Once I went out to the river. Spellbound, I watched its inscrutable face. There was a quiet enchanting thoughtfulness about it. I went down to the water and saw myself. A horrible mug with a beard. Wild, lonely eyes. I remember turning away in disgust.

I started looking around. I began to wonder who I was and what I was doing there. My past, my mishaps flashed before me. I saw myself, I saw Erik, Ruzhena, the biotosis, the council, the congress. I remembered everything, and I was ashamed. I was ashamed not for myself, a common, weak, and not very good man. I was ashamed of my intellect, my thoughts. The lofty ideas I worshipped, the beautiful ideals I dreamed about, had been turned to ashes by selfish, egotistical desire. I had gotten nowhere. I had given up at the most important moment, run off like a kid from the long difficult battle for our baby—our World Soul. It happened because my strength had been wasted on too many imaginary battles. They must have thought Ruzhena's death shattered me. The trouble was that it didn't. Ruzhena's death was the straw that broke the camel's back. But the back has to be loaded up to finally break.

I gradually turned into a regular hobo. My simple physical needs were easily satisfied. I understood that I was still on the road of loneliness and rejection. And I loved being on that road.

But then the scales fell from my eyes. I lost my gloomy disinterest. I knew what I had to do. I followed the river seven miles to the port. A small tug was hiring a new crew. I became the captain. My work was not difficult. I transported small barges carrying construction materials or fuel within my area. But I worked hard and well. I was a first-class captain, even if they didn't write about me in the papers.

All this happened before I found the Sardine Café. I was walking around Kuntsevo and came upon the old door by accident. I stood before it a long time, trying to decide whether I should go in. Some memory, a hint of something far away and very dear, stirred within me, and I went in. Then every time I was in Kuntsevo, I would go to the Sardine and drink heavily. The past would return to me, I became the old Sergei Arefyev. The captain's persona would fall from me like a carnival mask.

Sometimes there were other people in the café, but they usually did not return.

One night a fellow came in. We started talking. When I got very drunk, I recognized him and he recognized me. It was Erik. We were so terrified that it sobered us up. And we ran off immediately. I went back to the tug, and he went back to his hospital.

But the next day we were in the Sardine again. That continued until we learned to control our consciousness, until we could keep our memories firmly in hand. Soon we didn't need the Sardine's help. All that was needed was the willpower to keep ourselves in view. It wasn't easy, but we did it. I would have never escaped from prison if it hadn't been for Erik. Erik! Only then did I realize what he was. All that time it was I and not he who had basked in reflected glory.

It was particularly dangerous at night. The biotosis conquered us at night. We would prepare lists the night before of words and events that brought back our memories. It was a good thing there were two of us.

When Erik didn't show up for a few days, I would go to his place or to the hospital. He would look at me blankly and not recognize me. It was a hellish force that kept us apart. There was no room for me in the life that the biotosis had planned for him, and he did not remember about me. That was the story of those days. People's brains processed only "useful" information —that is, whatever applied to just functioning. By blocking out people's interest in anything not immediately useful and removing it from their sphere of attention, the World Soul reduced them to mindless cyborgs.

I would drag Erik out of the psychological quicksand that the World Soul had thrown him in, and we would resume training. Finally we managed to develop a system of thoughts, associations, and simple physical movements that guaranteed a normal state.

We decided to liquidate the biotosis. The problem seemed impossible at first. We couldn't blow it up. It was potentially fatal and threatened the psychological stability of the entire world. Erik knew from firsthand experience what touching the World Soul meant. The physical destruction of the biotosis might be accompanied by instantaneous death or madness for the entire world. And time was passing. The biotosis was growing stronger. We had to hurry. Every hour of consciousness cost us plenty.

"In order to destroy a psychological enemy like the biotosis," Erik told me, "we have to find its weak spots. We must go to Khokai-Rokh."

We got ready to go as fast as possible. We picked up the latest equipment from abandoned labs. I got my concentrator from the Institute of Telepathy, which had been abandoned by every employee—the World Soul went to a lot of trouble there! Erik wanted to use it in some experiments of his own.

It was strange to be walking on the dirty floor that had once sparkled, strange to see the garbage, the rundown condition of a building that only three months before had been filled with lively people who had argued and had ideas and talked.

I found my apparatus, dusty and rusty, in Ermolov's office. Spare crystals were locked in the big safe. There were also two boxes of tiny ruby crystals. Apparently, Ermolov had been planning to do something with them.

A few days later we were in Khokai-Rokh. We found Zaozersky there, almost completely wild, alone in the multistoried station. We spent a week resuscitating him, until he was back to normal. Then the three of us got to work.

And finally, we ran our first experiment. It was based on my concentrator. Erik reasoned like this:

"Your concentrator will function as a screen. It has to concentrate the diffused radiation of the biotosis and return it onto the body of the biotosis as a rectilinear beam. Then that part of the World Soul will be locked in on itself. It will then be out of the general energy flow disseminated by the biotosis. We have to see if my theory is right."

The experiment was dangerous, we knew that. But anything to do with the biotosis was dangerous.

I said that I would run the first experiment. Erik didn't want to agree for quite some time, but it was silly, because no one knew which was more dangerous, to be standing on the sidelines or near the equipment.

And the day came. It had snowed, but it was still warm, so the snow had melted. Erik and Zaozersky shook my hand and left. I aimed the reflector at the biotosis. I put on the helmet with all the stuff for emotional and physiological recording, moved the equipment closer and . . . I was stalling. My object was simple: to test whether the reflector let through the biotosis' rays and to record my sensations in detail. The recorder was already humming on my lap. The door slammed shut. They were gone. I glanced around one last time at the foggy mass of the biotosis and turned on the concentrator at maximum level. A lemon beam struck my eyes. And then everything disappeared.

I was walking on an earth where what we consider to be our future had become part of the distant past. I knew that capitalism, socialism, communism, and many other social formations that have no names in our dictionaries had come and gone.

The ground was amazingly smooth and flat. Where I was walking it felt like a smooth floor covered with a thick carpet of a springy grass that was unfamiliar to me. The sun was shining, and there wasn't a cloud in the sky. I was certain that the geometrical perfection of the landscape bespoke its artificial origins. I walked for a long time, and the landscape never changed. I did not come across rivers, or ravines, or forests. A monotonous green plain stretched as far as the eye could see. The sun was heading toward sunset, but it got no darker. A blue light came from the east, getting stronger, and when the sun went down, the plain was lit by the blinding blue light.

Suddenly I saw people soaring in the air. They were moving with great speed at an altitude of seven or eight yards above the ground. There were three of them. When they noticed me, they turned sharply off course toward me. They were far away, and I couldn't make out their faces. A great excitement overwhelmed me, my head spun, and I fell face down into the spicy grass, which had water sparkling under it.

I was awakened by a bright light in my eyes. I was on a litter. People were bent over me. At first I thought they were naked, but then I saw an almost invisible shiny covering on their bodies, like fish scales. The people looked like ordinary people. Tall, stately, and strong. Only they were completely hairless—no eyebrows, no eyelashes. They seemed strange to me, but I was infinitely happy to see that after a million years there were still people on the earth. I was amazed by their incredibly tiny mouths. The men and women resembled one another greatly. They looked like brothers and sisters. They had an odd beauty. They did not speak, but they exchanged glances and smiled.

I moaned. They left immediately and a thin man, an old man I thought, even though he moved like a youth, leaned over me. His penetrating gaze traveled along my face, body, and clothes. I felt that he was satisfied by the inspection. He smiled at me. His sharply delineated little lips spread apart and I saw his toothless mouth. It wasn't ugly in the least. I knew that that was the way it should be, that that's what the people of the distant future were like. I was thirsty and I told him. The old man seemed to be stunned by the sound of my voice. He moved away from me for a second. Then he carefully smoothed my forehead and cheeks. My thirst disappeared. Energy coursed through my body. I sat up and looked around.

I was in a long, roomy place, like a hangar. Light filtered in through the walls. People lay or sat in various positions on litters like mine. They conversed in silence. I could tell that they were communicating by the way they turned their heads and moved their hands. As I looked closer, I realized that there was one special thing about them. No one was lying on his litter the way I was, flat against it. They were all hovering in the air.

"Antigravitation." The word passed through my mind.

I walked over to the end of the hangar to the exit. No one restrained me or paid any attention to me, except for the old man, whom I had dubbed the physician, who watched me.

I went out. There were five other hangars on the left. I realized that they served as protection from the bright skies that had neither sun nor clouds. Probably their thin walls served some other purpose as well. Large red sparks danced on their silvery surfaces.

The town was situated in the bottom of a hollow. A transparent brook meandered at my feet. The area was uninhabited. I could see clumps of the bright-green grass above me. It overhung the precipice like lava, ready to pour in.

I saw two people. They appeared above the edge of the hollow, inscribed a semicircle in the air, and disappeared in the crevice from which I had just come. I felt that I had to follow them. But it had nothing to do with any conscious decision on my part.

The hangar was bustling. They had all flown up from their places and gathered around a dark object that looked like a chair. I sat in it and knew that I had acted properly. They put a mask on my face and fastened a shiny metallic hoop to my head. Then the physician carefully placed two cold metallic rods in my hands. Thin wires attached them to the chair's handrails. Nothing happened. I sat and held the sticks and they watched the hoop that was my crown. They were bunched together, and I observed them closely. I realized what was different about their body structure. They didn't have the rounded stomachs I was used to. Their rib cages ended in a depression that connected to their wasplike waists. And again I understood that that wasn't ugly, but right.

They were suddenly animated. Almost all of them opened their eyes wide. It was strange to see unfeigned human surprise on those immobile faces. They were looking at each other, nodding and shaking their heads. They seemed to have understood something about me. Then they freed me of the mask and crown. The chair evaporated. They all returned to their places on the litters.

The physician came up to me and put his hand on my shoulder. I got sleepy. I sat down, then lay down, and then fell asleep. My sleep was light and refreshing. When I awoke I found a vessel with a clear liquid at my feet. I thought it was water. I drank it and realized that I was wrong: I suddenly felt as full as if I had had a large meal.

The hangar was almost completely empty. No one but the physician was there. He came up to me and smiled. To tell the truth, that grin was beginning to irritate me. If that was the extent of future man's capabilities, well, I wasn't very impressed.

I pointed at my chest and said: "Sergei." The old man smiled and nodded. I was taken aback. He took me by the hand and led me into a corner of the hangar. There was the chair that I had been sitting on. The old man pointed at the metal hoop. He touched something on the chair, and I saw myself, Moscow, familiar faces, Erik, Ruzhena, Father, Lola, and some unclear wavy lines on top and bottom in the hoop. It was all moving so fast that I couldn't follow it.

They had recorded all the information in my brain. They knew everything about me. But how could I find out anything about them? I could see them, touch them, but.... The people of the future are strange. They are unusually gentle and tender. Maybe that's just a mirage created by their silence, constant smiles, and noiseless movements. I don't know, but I felt as though I were part of a very intense pantomime.

The old man looked troubled. He glanced at me anxiously and floated to the exit. I ran after him. The town was unrecognizable. The inhabitants of all six hangars had come outside. They were crowding around, if that term can be applied to people hovering in air at various heights.

A dark spot appeared on the horizon. It grew, and soon I saw that it was a group of several people. They were carrying lumps of a light, formless mass.

They put down their burden on a light-colored plastic sheet spread on the ground. The three pieces of a material unknown to me riveted everyone's attention for some reason. They fluttered around excitedly, but no one crossed the boundaries of the light-blue square.

I went up to them to see what was happening. The lumps looked like badly butchered animal carcasses. There were drops of blood on the rosy skin. The lumps were about the size of full-grown calves. They thrashed about but couldn't move from their places. The strange stubs on their sides, resembling feelers, flopped helplessly on the plastic. One of the lumps managed to turn over; it faced me. I was horrified. Two huge human eyes looked at me. So it was human? Those were people? I wanted to run, but my feet were glued to the ground, and my eyes drank in every detail. A huge head taking up half the body, pale eyes, no ears, a barely outlined mouth, and a disgustingly formless body with undeveloped extremities.

My physician and another man went up to them. They began washing the lumps with a golden liquid. I could smell alcohol. The lumps squirmed and made a noise that sounded like a pig's grunts. I watched the men's gentle movements with a shudder. I thought just touching those embryos, with their independent existence, was horrible. The people from the hangars were like Greek gods compared to the stumps.

The physician and his helpers dressed the new arrivals. They pulled a thin, scaly covering on their bodies. The stumps' bleeding stopped, and now they looked like tightly diapered overgrown infants. They were stood on end, and they no longer flopped over helplessly. Apparently, the scales had some antigravitational property.

Then the entire crowd, which had been observing the proceedings in silence, floated over to them with silent smiles. An indistinct muttering came in reply. The cripples' faces were distorted by wild grimaces. Perhaps they were trying to smile back.

After a while the lumps were taken back to the hangars in total silence. I was alone.

I was trying to comprehend what had happened. Where did those pathetic creatures come from? What made the people from the hangars treat them with such tender care? Could the entire civilization of the future be concentrated here in these six hangars made of semitranslucent material? That couldn't be. Somewhere far from here a battle was raging, and its weak echoes were heard here. But I decided to exploit the situation to the hilt. I returned to the hangar and tried to make logical contact with its smiling inhabitants. That turned out to be a difficult proposition.

The smiling ones watched my attempts attentively, but did not react. My excursions into the elementary axioms of mathematics and biology elicited no response. I was too far removed from them. I reminded myself of a puppy trying to communicate with his masters by squealing. The condescending smiles did not disappear from my listeners' faces. I was tired of talking and counting on my fingers, so I shut up.

I was fast asleep when I was awakened by definite jabs. There were several people next to my litter. They were wearing dark masks that covered their faces and heads. They took off my worn clothes and wrapped me in a scaly covering. The plastic adhered to my skin.

Then they pointed to the exit. I pushed off from the floor and rose in the air, but I couldn't move the way my companions did. I tumbled around under the ceiling, grabbed hold of the slippery walls, and marked time in place. They tied a long yellow metal towline to me, and we set off.

It was still daytime, but now I could see the sun. It shone in the cloudless sky, and I found its even diffused light very pleasant. The sun was as I had known it, millions of years ago.

We flew up out of the hollow and headed north. From the low altitude at which we were flying, the earth looked like a gigantic concave cup. Bright-green grass, shimmering opalescently, and nothing else. The view was boring. It felt as though we hadn't advanced a foot. Only the grassy hillocks falling away below us gave proof of our forward motion.

We flew for a very long time. The sun disappeared, my only friend in this world, and we floated under the glowing sky. Once in a while, one of them would descend to the ground and return with a vessel of silvery moisture. I drank it, and that was my food and water. I don't know what the others fed on. Maybe they needed less food than I did. Who knows? They were kind to me, those smiling gods, but I didn't understand them.

I thought about things as I flew along. So that's what you're like, supercivilized Earth! Man has shaped you for his convenience. He razed the mountains and filled in the seas. And then I thought that the grass was simply an unknown species of seaweed, which made it impossible to guess whether there was land or water under it. Man plucked the clouds from the sky and forced the atmosphere to glow. He leveled the ground so that it resembled a football field and made the climate the same throughout the globe. And probably the humidity was also strictly regulated to ensure maximum comfort for the human body.

In their relentless striving for conformity, order, and control, people had turned the planet into an apartment decorated strictly in one style. The monotony of the style made me think that there had to be only one homeowner. But who? Not my smiling ones? I looked at them and noticed a change in their expressions.

The smiles were gone. Their tiny mouths were compressed into short lines. Their eyes blazed with excitement. Large red sparks flew from their masks. The smiling ones picked up speed, pulling the towline taut.

New groups of smiling ones joined us from the right and left. I knew that they had been waiting for us in the grass below. They looked like mine, but were distinguished either by the color of their scales or by their masks. I noticed several females among the new arrivals. They were all excited and tense. The flight kept speeding up, and I felt hot.

There was a roar up ahead. It sounded like thunder. I thought that we were approaching a volcano, but discounted the thought immediately: how could there be a volcano on such a well-ordered planet?

My traveling companions were filling in the formation. The distance between them was diminishing. We were flying in a thick cloud.

And then I saw a pale-pink haze on the horizon. Something was glittering in it. Long tongues of a rosy white mass licked the green field below us. Farther on, the tongues blended into a solid, rolling field. It was smoking and rumbling.

We descended. The ocean of the wriggling rosy material was made up of the lumps. Each lump was tightly pressed to his neighbors, with only a barely visible line between them. We were flying at what I thought was a dangerously high speed, close to their top limit. The green peninsulas and grass islands disappeared, and there was only the rolling living fabric beneath us. I was certain that it was alive without having any evidence to confirm it.

It was terrifying to look at my companions. Stony faces, clenched jaws, tense, excited eyes. In a tight group, we flew on.

I think a lot of time passed. I was very tired and could barely stay up. They had taken off my towline, and I was flying squeezed in from four sides by the firm bodies of the smiling ones. (The term seemed particularly inappropriate just then.)

The same foamy reddish waves stretched out below us. Someone who had been flying below me moved up, and I had a better view. I could watch what was directly below me.

The lumps that constituted the mass were taking on clearer features. They had additional lines, and something about them troubled me. It felt like....

Slowly getting cold, I stared into the wavy sea shimmering below me. But my companions flew up sharply, and we flew at an altitude from which I could no longer make out the lumps. I began nudging my companions and pointing down. One of them carefully smoothed my forehead and cheeks. My anxiety abated. But as soon as we descended, it came back. I had goosebumps the size of a fist.

The lumps that made up the sea were people! There were hundreds of thousands, millions of people, squeezed together tightly. Now I could clearly see the outlines of their heads, their eyesockets, and weakly developed ears. Some of them waved the stubs they had for arms. Some followed our swift flight with a lazy turn of the head.

A billion-headed animal, or creature, or supercreature. I was flying over a human sea, over a society-organism that had a single body, and each one of them was merely a cell. A scream caught in my throat.

Events unfolded abruptly and unexpectedly. Our flight braked sharply. The smiling ones, and I along with them, made an arc in the air. We were there. It was probably not far from here to the central part, to the Master of the planet. I examined the human heads below us—formless, flabby, indefinite, almost eye-less—and I was sickened.

Suddenly two of the smiling ones swooped down. They fell into the human ocean and began to struggle with one of the heads. When they flew up again a few minutes later, a bloody lump was struggling and squealing in their arms. It was picked up by two other smiling ones, who flew south with it. The smil-ing ones swooped down again and repeated the operation. A dark space opened below, showing the green grass where the lumps had been. Our ranks were thinning. One after another, in twos and threes, the smiling ones headed back, carrying with them the trembling bodies of people torn from the human ocean. It was hard on the remaining ones. Sweat streamed down their masked faces. Their movements were becoming more and more nervous and hurried. The masks and helmets were in flames. Rivers of sparks poured down from them onto the scaly bodies of the smiling ones.

One of the hunters flew up to me and pointed down. I under-stood that they were offering me a chance to tear out a pathetic human lump from the seething mass below. I obeyed and after a few clumsy attempts, flew down into the dark vortex. When I touched the firm green seaweed exposed by the removal of the bodies, I felt a strange weakness. At first only one thing was clear to me—a total absence of desires. I wanted only to lie down, stretch out, and lose myself in a sweet dream. Then in my dreamlike stupor I sensed pride and happiness, totally unex-pected in these circumstances. I knew that they weren't my feel-ings. They belonged to the ocean of life that I had fallen into. They were created by a single field of world reason that had bound billions of people into a single organism. I had completely forgotten the reason for my descent. I forgot the smiling ones. I forgot everything. I was troubled by new thoughts and feelings that took my breath away. They were vague, blurred, but very strong. I was slowly drowning in the ocean of thoughts.

I made my way carefully toward the trembling naked bodies that no longer seemed disgusting or hostile. Something happened up above. I looked up and saw a smiling one. Arms outstretched, he fell. When he got close to the ground, he slowly removed his mask and helmet.

I rushed up to him. Several bounds brought me above the rumbling heads. I flew up to the smiling one, but it was too late. He had been sucked in. I pulled at his arms and shook him by the shoulders in vain. He kept sinking into the human quagmire. He did not want to leave any more. The sea of heads rumbled in pleasure.

I looked around and saw the receding figures of the smiling ones. They were taking a few more pathetic squealing lumps with them. I flew after.

Our return was even more difficult and longer than the flight to the Master. Exhaustion racked every pore, every cell in my body. Some unknown force held us back, hindered our movements, and distracted us from concentrating.

The faces of the smiling ones went from bronze to ash-gray. They performed the small, complicated moves that guaranteed a steady flight. It was more difficult for me, because I had trouble remembering the techniques of flight: shaking my head, moving my lips, smiling. The position and speed of the body depended on those grimaces.

By the time we sighted the hollow where the six hangars nestled in the sun, I had mastered the simple tricks of flying.

We were greeted by the town's entire populace, and the new human bodies were washed. I would have been ashamed to call them stumps now.

Then we slept. It felt as if I slept a year, it was so deep and good.

When I came out of the hangar the first things I saw were the people from the Master's body. They were being taught to walk. I was struck by the change in their appearance. They had developed definition and concreteness. Their round heads were raised up on necks and their eyes had opened, like little blue windows. The rosy skin was turning dark, burnished with a bronze tint. They were beginning to look like the smiling ones. Even their little mouths twisted into a grimace that looked like a grin. And I thought, Did the flying squads of the smiling ones come from these pieces torn from the human ocean? But who were the flying ones? Why were they carrying on their cruel, never-ending battle with the society-organism that inhabits our earth? Thousands of questions bombarded my brain. I couldn't answer a single one. But I did know one thing:

The development of human society had led to the creation of an organism that bound people together on some complex principles that I did not understand. The planet had been studied, mastered, and equipped to such an extent that there were no material questions that needed solving. The age of inorganic materials, metals, and machines had long passed. The earth had become a bioplanet. Everything was solved with the aid of molecular and biochemical relations. The society-organism that lived on earth had properties I could not fathom. I had been present at a battle between the smiling ones and this ocean of human consciousness, and I understood neither the aims nor the methods of the war.

Perhaps I had witnessed the clash of two branches of evolution, distinguished by the tendencies of their development?

Perhaps. But I was on a level that did not permit me even to understand the aims of these perfected organisms. After all, the struggle between man, society, and the smiling ones took place in regions of thought that I could not begin to fathom. All I knew for sure was that the battles did take place. No wonder there were sparks flying constantly on the hangar walls. Maybe they fought with thoughts the way we used to fight with fists? I remembered the smiling one swallowed up by the Ocean of Life. Strangely enough, I no longer felt revulsion for the waves of swaying human heads. Having been among them, I understood that it was a completely different kind of life and that we couldn't measure it by our limited standards. Had they acquired the universal happiness of legend? But then why weren't the smiling ones with them? Or were antagonism and conflict the inevitable companions of the highest forms of consciousness just as they were of the lowest?

"Only now do I see the real horror of the biotosis," Ermolov said, turning off the tape recorder and removing the cassette.

Erik relieved the heavy oppressive silence that followed.

"We carried Sergei back here, and he managed to make the

tape before he died. So we've had time to think it over. I . . . let Oleg tell you."

Zaozersky rubbed his bearded cheek. He walked around the room, then sat on the bed.

"It's not only that the tape let us look into the depths of the biotosis. The World Soul has put powerful ammunition into our hands."

"What do you think?" Karabichev interrupted. "What is this phantasmagoria? Sergei's euphoric vision or the result of the biotosis' action?"

"It's hard to say. Probably some of both. The section of the biotosis that was closed off onto itself unleashed a shower of beams on Sergei that revealed information about the future. The biotosis is a cyclopedic computer without a psyche or consciousness of its own. The information about the future is created by purely logical, and therefore incorrect, extrapolation from the present. The human sea that the biotosis created, in which all individuality is dissolved, runs against human nature. A future like that is abhorrent. It is senseless and impossible. That goes without saying. All that is clear, more or less. But there is something else. Why did the biotosis give that information in response to excitation?

"If it had a consciousness, a rational mind, it would be hard to answer the question. There would be many possibilities. But the World Soul is a machine, a living logic machine, connected with a feedback mechanism to our consciousness. And the picture it painted of the 'future' is nothing more than a primitive defense reaction to physical irritation. It showed the society that would best suit the biotosis. The master of the planet in such a society-organism would be the biotosis itself. People would have to give up all vestiges of individuality. And then they would create a unified, calm background of emanations that were most conducive for the development of the biotosis. It has to both separate people, the way it did with us biologists, and unite them, docile and passive, into a single substance that gives off an even radiation. Only then it will be safe from any threat to its physical integrity. And it did all this automatically, on the level of cybernetics, and not on the level of inductive and deductive reasoning.

"Once we realized that, it was not difficult to come up with a plan to fight the biotosis. We must counter separation with unity, the unification of people who have set themselves the goal of struggle against the biotosis. And the more of us there are, the worse it will be for the World Soul. It was created from the brain energy of the people of the entire world. These were people of different convictions, desires, and goals. And they created a certain average background that turned out to be so conducive to the biotosis' growth. But what if we unite the people? And direct all their thoughts to fighting the biotosis? What then?"

"Then it will die," Erik said. "A separated humanity created it, and a united one will destroy it."

"Yes, united humanity will destroy it." Zaozersky stood up and walked around the room once more. "United mankind! Not fused together physically into an amorphous human sea, but bound by a single idea."

"Today that uniting idea must be the struggle against the biotosis," Erik said.

Ermolov laughed. Erik and Zaozersky looked at him in surprise.

"Please don't pay any attention, I'm just thinking," Ermolov explained. "You're absolutely marvelous people. And that's a fact. And remember, you're not alone. The movement against the effects of the biotosis is growing stronger all over the world. The rockets on the satellite—that's only a last resort. We believe that we'll be able to overcome the biotosis without them. If you only knew how many people blocked by the biotosis have learned to control their own wills! Our goal is to direct and organize this new movement. Lead the people into battle for the future. For a human future!"

He is only a voice, eternally captured in the sounds of this tape. From century to century, generation to generation, he bears the tale of events in which he himself took part. The World Soul was wrong. And its errors were inevitable, since it could only shuffle human memories mechanically.

People listen to him carefully, but suspiciously. And they are right. But people should know more than what was or will be. They must know that which must never be. He comes alive when people come to him, his distant descendants. They come to him with the sun, which slides along the walls in a blurred yellow spot. The hot, happy sun. The sun of a happy world built by the hands of his contemporaries.

About the Authors

Mikhail Emtsev is a physicist. Eremei Parnov is a chemist. They began writing science fiction in 1959. Their other books include *Clumps of Darkness on the Needle of Time* and *The Sea of Dirac*.

About the Translator

ANTONINA W. BOUIS has translated five books, three plays, and numerous articles for magazines and newspapers. She recently spent several months in Moscow working for American network television.

About the Series

In the Soviet Union, as in the U.S.A., the fascination with the possibilities of science and technology has lead to a rich and long tradition of science fiction. Macmillan's BEST OF SOVIET SCIENCE FICTION is now presenting the major works in lively, readable translations, allowing the American reader to explore—for the first time—the wide range of visions of space, time, and man's future in the other major S-F tradition.